Laura A. S. Nourse

The Lyric of Life

Laura A. S. Nourse

The Lyric of Life

ISBN/EAN: 9783744784092

Printed in Europe, USA, Canada, Australia, Japan

Cover: Foto ©Andreas Hilbeck / pixelio.de

More available books at **www.hansebooks.com**

THE
LYRIC OF LIFE

UNFOLDING

PRINCIPLES OF IMMORTALITY IN THE SEEN
AND UNSEEN FORCES OF NATURE

NEW THOUGHT IN PLANETARY MOTION
AND
THE WORLD LIFE OF SUNS

BY LAURA A. SUNDERLIN NOURSE

Author of Pencilings from Immortality

Reason was given that its light
Might radiate surrounding night

AUTHOR'S EDITION

BUFFALO
CHARLES WELLS MOULTON
1892

Printed by C. W. Moulton, Buffalo, N. Y.

PREFACE.

When life was first made explainable to me, why a personal body, my instructors of thought claimed that forces were individualized with atoms similar to physical aggregations of matter.

That all forces, whether electricity, oxygen, magnetism, or whatever force finding expression in Nature, those forces were composed of atoms of an invisible nature. And to individualize a physical form, an atom of invisible nature always came in contact with matter, and, held by its inertia, by self-expansion, grew larger in form and materialized atoms of matter into forms.

They also told me that the planets' revolution of life was effective by its internal heat, and that scientists had overlooked the simple force of motion that caused the revolution of planets on their axis by the heat engendered in bodies shaped as worlds, having this peculiarity of their own involuntary motion.

These truths embodied in this work came to me after much thought and mental questionings, in the year 1879, solving what life was in all its varied forms of personality.

This theory being new, it was difficult to gain admittance sufficient to explain in newspaper articles published since at various times and seasons, therefore, in 1881, I published a leaflet embodying this theory, that it might be productive of thought on a new line of reasoning-life embodied always in the atom prior to physical existence. In the same year I also published an article in the "Boston Investigator," carrying out the same line of thought, in reply to an article upon the " Seen and Unseen " in Nature, taking the position in demonstration of the "unseen."

But as all new theories are slow to action, the thought conceived in my mind to put them into book form, for which the " Lyric of Life " has been written, thinking in this way condensed to be better than in lengthy articles of MSS. preserved that had not yet found their way to press. Since much bearing upon the same line of thought is now advocated by the various writers of to-day, I hope to be better understood by the world of thought and aid the work of proving the immortality of the soul upon principles of science.

THE AUTHOR.

INTRODUCTION.

My mind conceived this Lyric of our life
Long years ago, when thought, in constant strife,
Was questioning to unfold a proof to me
Reasonable—of all immortality
Through Nature's labyrinths of endless shade;
Reveal—what through my poem I have made
To feebly show the light—revealed to mind;
And let some other one more thoughtful, find
The links expressive for our use,
That I have undiscovered, to produce.—
The origin and growth of every human mind,
And endless chain of life of every kind;
That are immortal—because all life must be
An atom life—from that of Deity,
That fills the universe with life and mind,
Expressed in atom lives of every kind.
Primevally combined in energy and forces;
That throughout the Universal Whole are life resources;
One grand vast mechanism of endless power;
Whose unity of presence seems like our
Body, ever present with a soul,
That universal acts with mind control;
The seat of mind its central power and source,
And thus we see the Universe of central force.

All within it, moving 'round some Grand Stupenduous Whole,
Some unseen center filled with life and soul;
Some energy of ever central call.
Attraction in its love through all in all;
A unit power of mind through all within,—
Father and Mother Life—a Dual One;
And for a better name Him was begun:
And like our body it is atom filled,
And each inherently intelligence instilled;
Mind atoms that inherent from the source,
Has love's attraction, as their central force.
To individualize a larger mind would be,
Growing conscious individuality;
And has that love within from the Divine,
A spark of it to elevate the mind,
And bear it upward in the ever ceaseless range
Of life and motion through progressive change,
Of beauty harmony and all fullness find,
In perfect living with harmonious mind.
Can there be ending, who could ending solve?
When universal motion doth revolve,
And progress bears us upward as a flower,
Unfolding leaf by leaf reveals to our
Eternal blossoming of the mind—disclose
The constant fullness of the perfect rose;
So that which always is and never dies,
Must higher circles in progression rise;
And distance in its length no thought can span,
Or can it be conceived by life in man.

CONTENTS.

THE LYRIC OF LIFE.

LAURA A. SUNDERLIN NOURSE,

THE LYRIC OF LIFE.

IN the archives of all Nature,
  The hidden life of every creature,
Existed in the "Great All Source,"
As atoms of its central force;
And so a force each life expressed,
As it individually progressed.

"Down in Nature's hiding places
  Atoms leap with sudden graces;
  Now released from rock and mud,
  Up they troup to lily's bud;
  And from the upper brightness
  It draws its own pure whiteness,
  And comes to be
  A symbol of the things we cannot see.
  Thus the hidden soul of things"
  Unseen, a revelation brings;
  Thus the law to all the living,
  This same growth of life is giving.
  Just an Atom in its start,
  Pulses with a central heart;
  Expanding as it larger grew,
  In its identity of you.

As it burst from foldings where
It breathed in something from the air;
And light received into the mind,
Responsive thought burst forth to shine;
Gaining each while added power,
As from a bud springs forth the flower.
Thus from atoms filling spaces,
Life develops different graces,
In the grand stupendous whole,
Swerved by Infinite control.
If a mental atom force,
Parts of God are we of course;
Atoms of His Infinite Mind,
Every life of every kind
That doth a unit life express,
Energy and thoughtfulness ;
Atoms all within His being,
Which compose the "Great All-Seeing" ;
Atoms are personal we know
And would be personal to grow ;
They in Nature always are,
Filling spaces,—or a star
May combine them in its force,
But released again, the Source,
Holds them in its body still,—
The Universe with atoms filled,
And individual forms would grow
From their central force we know ;
Atoms all within His being
Which compose the "Great All-Seeing."

As a body moves each part
Of the muscles, nerves and heart ;
Some more sensitive to heart motion ;
Respond to mind and God devotion ;
Feel the impulses and thrills,
Which God's love throughout all fills ;
For of atoms may be those,
That more sensitive parts compose,
In God's body which we build,
With created atoms filled.
Then to blame, O, who would be,
If a God they could not see !
Yet through varied circulation,
They will yet reach in creation,
Parts of God's stupendous form,
Where to new thought they are born ;
Then more active they would be
With all in Immensity,
Just as atoms forming nerves,
With the mind more sensitive serves ;
Atoms forming bone, more dull
To sensations of the whole,
And if parts of God are we,
In His likeness we may be.

First we see a mental force ;
An atom mind from mental source,
But growing larger comes to be
Conscious individuality.
Atoms centralized are things

Which a force together brings ;
Atoms all substances conceal,
This microscopes reveal ;
An atom is a unit power,
If individual grows,—each hour
More added power its growth expresses,
And what inherent it possesses,
Is manifested, as the bloom
In the plant expresses soon ;
So life breathing motion gains,
As unfoldment on explains.
If we see atoms draw together
By a force upon them, whether
That force is unseen or not,
That unseen a body's got,
If it shapes those things in one,
And a person does become.
If this force that doth combine,
Leaves it which we call the mind,
Leaves the body it has builded,
For a brighter life more gilded ;
Atoms then dissolve that made
Bodies that in substance stayed.
So we see the mind in force,
In a body first, of course ;
And it clothed itself and motion,
From the atoms in commotion,
That it could unto it draw,
By the force of love—it saw,
Were conditions to unfold,

As the earth in darkness holds
Just a little while the seed,
Till it bursts its shell and speeds
" Upward into higher brightness,
As the lily gains its whiteness,"
From the air, the dew and sun,
After it from darkness sprung,
With a body to adorn,
That unfolds its life and form,
Shape of what that life may be,
Whose motion we can only see,
Through the body up to build
Atoms, all of which is filled
With material atoms, drawn
By its love-revealing form.

Atom lives fill all the spaces,
All have different forms and places ;
All eternal still to grow
From their self start here below,
As an individual thing,
And the inward outward bring.
All and every kind immortal,
To build up each part and portal ;
Where that each may enter in,
Is unknown to all but Him ;
Of whose body we compose,
Of whose presence all yet know
As through fields of time progressed,
May the present each divest ;

Where we stand to-day another
May be standing yet—a brother,
And where others may have stood,
We may stand and be more good,
May reach heights of thought sublime,
That with dazzling radiance shine,
And unfold a blossom rare,
From those fields of upper air,
That will rival in its whiteness
More than all things known of brightness ;
Sparkling gems of thought perfume,
Sweeter than all known-of bloom,
When we rise from earth and clay
In the upper air of day ;
Daylight we have never known,
Only as we call our own,
Backward from the land of bliss
And comparing theirs with this ;
For no language we have may
Express that of theirs, they say—
Nature's land of bloom and flowers,
Just above this land of ours.

HOW EVIL IS UNGROWTH.

IF you say that all is God,
    Every life that ever trod ;
God make evil then, I hear
Some one asking, it is queer !
Just compare the human mind

To an instrument whose kind
Of notes produce harmonious sound,
But if vacant notes are found,
On the keyboard, you will hear
Discord ; so evils appear
In our actions till each note
Of the mind is full by rote ;
Grown to fullness and enwrought
To produce harmonious thought.
Cramped, that mind may have begun,
By conditions from which it sprung.
As the green fruit on the tree,
By simply living, yet will be
Sweetest fruit, and may combine
All the flavor of its kind ;
So with all life yet be growing
Until no evil we are knowing.
By development we find
All the beauty of the mind.

HIDDEN FORCES.

ATTRACTION is all present in the air ;
It attracts together everywhere
A fluid, in a body round—
A rain drop or a bubble found
To be a miniature of worlds ;
Or lead made so if it unfurls
In melted particles through space.
This something filling every place,

ttracts them round, as you will see,
Attraction everywhere must be ;
In everything we breathe or know,
This element that does not show,
Must be all present everywhere,
A substance filling all the air ;
And everywhere through boundless space ;
To hold the planets in their place,
And electricity must combine
With it and others we can find,
Just as invisible in space,
Which science finds in every place.
For in the contents of your room
It generates and would assume
Its presence, as well as anywhere
In distant space or in the air ;
Attraction tends to organize
Its movements cannot this disguise.

ATTRACTION UNCHANGEABLE IN NATURE.

ATTRACTION goes through intense cold
To reach the earth from pole to pole ;
From sun to earth, the space between,
Would destroy all substance—seen
Like a material, but not so
With attraction in its flow,
Its identity remains.
Through heat and cold, 'tis just the same.
Electricity is not found

Through all temperatures around
The world, to change its identity ;
The same results we always see ;
If it should change that could not be ;
Material things would be unlike,
And variable would disunite ;
If cold and heat would meet their way,
The law of change they would obey,
And life, we find its nature, too,
Alike in all of nature through,
Invariable,—it will produce
Thoughts, as results in every use
That its activity is seen ;
Its breathing motion is—we mean
Expressed in the results of thought,
When action with the mind is wrought
With what the air contains,—you see
The chemistry of thought will be.

HYPNOTISM DEMONSTRATES THE INVISI-
BILITY OF MIND.

MIND is a something you must know,
As it, invisible, will go
Across the room,—it is not seen,
And your subject moved has been
With your thought—and you will do
That thought that went from him to you ;
You were blind and did not see ;
So not material the thought could be,

For it passed through your head to you,
To reach your mind and make you do
Just as your will would do for fact,
If it upon yourself did act ;
If it went through his material there
And on to you, through space and air,
When in silence sent to you
His thought that you received to do.
Invisible you see mind force ;
And is a unit power, of course ;
If it is natural so—as ever
Will it not be the same forever ?
It is a force like all ethereal,
Unchanging through conditions of the material.
And is it not this power of mind
That spirit friends with us entwine
Their thoughts with ours, and make us do ?
Mesmeric thought from them to you,
When you reach out your thoughts to them,
A line of means you have with them ?
The mind unchanging is ethereal,
Holds its identity through changed material,
No matter how the body may
Be with disease, or health, or gray
With age, or buoyant youth expressed ;
Mind acts with thought the more or less ;
And thus we see there is refined,
Unseen—with elements of mind
In Nature, that unchanged will be
Through cold and heat variety.

The same as Attraction polar draws
Toward the north, unchanging cause ;
And thus we reason Nature holds
Unchanging tendencies of things untold ;
With reason, comprehension too,
We thus can bring the unseen to view ;
The unseen elements will flow,
Through a material substance go.
Thus magnetism in the stone,
Gives to the knife-blade of its own ;
And both will then the needle draw
Through a material substance there ;
A spirit substance will declare ;
Will go right through material seen,
As life permeates between
The substance of material forms,
As in the knife-blade there performs,
A substance that material fills,
Imparted to it as our wills
Of life, will move a body, too,
And permeate it through and through ;
While ours is personal in thought,
Magnetism is like a substance wrought ;
That will express its nature there
Invisible, unchanging where
It occupies material space,
And never seems to take its place ;
No more than a drop of water will make
A lump of sugar larger take
Its form, by adding, it would be

No larger in its form to see.
So life may occupy space between
Atomic structures, that is seen,
But so infinitesimal that to view
It seems a perfect solid to
Us, but then 'tis porous through
A miscroscope—atomic view,
In every part of every grade ;
The physical body, it is made.
The spiritual body may be so
That clothes the mind while it doth grow ;
For every atom doth combine,
Touched by its spiritual, with mind ;
That central force in atoms seen,
Is spiritual and what we mean,
And when the mind a body made,
Out of materials every grade,
The spirit atom in them through,
Would make a spirit body, too.

THE USE OF A MATERIAL BODY.

LIFE self-motion will assert ;
    But it must first be held inert ;
If in selfhood it would grow ;
In material atom so
It was bound, a central force
In life's progress upward course.
The positive and negative atom unite
In one electrical circle of power.

In the union so combined,
We possess a dual mind ;
As two things will come to be
One in personality ;
Two eyes blend into one sight,
So doth two in one unite ;
So doth two lobes of the brain
Unite one intellect the same,
And two atoms thus combine,
In the chemistry of mind ;
Making just one form we see
Natural to personality ;
Because two personals combine
Natural union of a mind,
Personal both as its source
Feels a nature as one force ;
The principals of female and male,
That in all Nature as one prevail,
Thus one moving force combine ;
Union of one moving mind,
The two natures move as one,
Naturally as one become ;
An individual form would grow
From this natural force we know ;
If they burst their atom cell,
As the seed will larger swell
And send upward to a tree,
What that seed contained to be ;
Through selections which it drew
Revealed the physical to view ;

And individual life expressed,
A unit form in matter dressed,
With atoms of materials bound,
When life the physical had found ;
And why materials came to be
A person of individuality.
You see the mind, its form and grade,
By growth of physical it made ;
Inharmonious shapes are so
Parts of mind that cannot grow ;
If conditions it had got
All affinitizing not ;
So the mental atom mind
Is inherent, yet you'll find
Of its species to unfold ;
Its conditions, too, are told ;
When it bursts its prison cell,
And unwraps itself so well,
With a body to adorn,
That unfolds its shape and form,
Shape of what that life will be
Moving on eternally.
You see the mind's mesmeric power
Is something invisible in our
Elements thrown off from mind ;
Thought transference, too, you find,
Is something invisible, unseen,
That passes from that mind between
The two, and makes the other do
Their will, is this attraction, too ?

This shows a hidden force the same ;
And mind attraction will explain
That mind was once an atom force,
From that of Universal Source,
Or would its nature be to bind,
And to it attract some other mind ?
The stronger to subserve the one,
That yielding to it did become
Moved, by the power—another mind
That through attraction thus did bind ;
Or by its hate, the law repel ;
Finds its expression, too, as well ;
To individualize itself, you know,
Attraction helps it larger grow ;
And draws material to combine—
The physical, by power of mind,
Secreted in itself to grow,
And larger individualize it—so
Natural as Universal Mind
That doth all worlds within it bind.

SEEN BY COMPREHENSION.

IS not attraction something seen,
   When it will hold with strength between
Two worlds, more strong than any power
Of a material, which in our
Knowledge could more stronger pull,
Than this of which all space is full ?
And if a substance will we find

That it is atomically combined,
As all material substance bound
Up in atoms, will be found ;
Attraction, you must plainly see,
Is not electricity, for we
Can tell their difference this way :
One through glass will go, we say,
While the other cannot go
Through the pane of glass, we know ;
Hence their difference is plain,
They cannot be both the same.
Both are substances unseen,
Whose presence moves, and it would seem
That something must be there to stir
An object, and I would prefer
To know if it would not be found,
Like all substances, atomic bound ?
Each atom natural to be
Invisible, like mind, in thee,
That as a unit moves like force,
And if attraction was the source
From which it sprung to larger life ?
Its unit mind-force growing more
And larger than it was before,
It manifested higher power,
And added motion, as in our
Growth of personality ;
Our life shows what it grows to be,
When it grew larger to begin
To show intelligence within ;

And breathing motion-life assume,
A consciousness to life illume
With thoughts, peculiar to its own,—
Results from larger motion grown,
From where it began itself to grow
From something like attraction that we know
To be a universal love,
By which all worlds doth move above ;
Love is a sentiment of mind ;
And has inherent thoughts combined
Within an atom of its force,
That doth reveal, mind is its source ;
And Love that moves all worlds entwined
In universal bonds is Mind ;
A finer element we see
Than moving electricity ;
But this is also just the same
A force invisible again,
Composed of atoms which will explain
The source of vegetable life forms ;
Their life growth just like ours performs ;
But opposite to us must be ;
Their life exhales oxygen to thee,
And carbonic gas, which we exhale
To them, is life, and so you see,
A complement for each are we.

IS ATTRACTION ATOMIC BECAUSE IT
SEPARATES?

WE know attraction in the stone
    Will to the knife-blade impart its own ;
And both will be attraction force
When separated from the source.
Attraction has by this explained,
That it of atoms is contained ;
That it is substance like the rest,
That has atomic been expressed,
Because it separates the same,
As coarser substance we could name ;
As coarser substance said to be
Atomic from this cause, so we
Can critically, from this cause, claim
Attraction must be just the same,
Of atoms bound, to disunite,
When love more strong attracts them quite
Out of the lode-stone, both possessed
Attraction separate expressed,
And both would draw the needle through
This element unseen to view.

FORCES ASSOCIATED IN THE SUN-RAY.

'TWAS found to be upon the " plate,"
   When scientists a ray did take,
Connected with " galvanometer coil"
And " gridiron wire," and found that all,
Through " Breguet's helix*," was displayed,
Four elements the sun-ray made ;
All associated as one,
That come to us in ray of sun,
The needles, deflected, found the force
Of electricity in sun-ray source ;
Circulating through the wires ;
Magnetism in the coil ;
And heat within the helix bound,
And motion next in needles found.
What was this motion, was it mind,
With the three other things combined,
Contained within the sun-ray force ?
Mind germs combined, a force would show,
Invisible in nature, too.

*"An elegant instrument formed by a coil of two metals, the unequal expansion of which indicates slight changes in temperature—the other extremities of the galvanometer and helix are connected by a wire and the needles brought to zero. As soon as a beam of either daylight or the oxy-hydrogen light is, by raising the shutter, permitted to impinge upon the plate the needles deflected. Thus light being the initiating force, we get chemical action on the plate, electricity circulating through the wires, magnetism in the coil, heat in the helix, and motion in the needles. Experiments of Prof. W. R. Grove, found in a work entitled 'Correlation and Conservation of Forces,' **page** 116—a work by Edward L. Yomans."

MIND NATURAL TO MOTION.

MIND is the only thing
        From rest a motion will begin ;
From perfect rest, will awake and be
Itself in action simply free ;
A motion set up and begin
Itself, so natural within.
And so we reason this may show
A force of motion natural so ;
Contained in elements of sun,—
The fountain source—all life-germs sprung ;
If it is mind, we have the source
Of life-germs in attractive force.
If life-germs in it, is explained,
What sunlight elements contained ;
Why flowers will bud and bloom if where
The sunshine falls upon them there,
And in the shade will grow and be
Without a bud or flower to see,
The sunshine falls upon the earth,
And fills it with life-germs for the birth
Of bud and bloom up to arise,
And question us with the surprise,
We often feel when there is grown,
New life where never seed is sown ;
And after this those forms contain
Those reproductive germs,—explained
In offspring, the same species—kind,
That each attract similar of mind,

To that of which its life contains,
And heredity in all explains ;
And this same law to all that live,
Has found the source that life doth give ;
Has found it in the rays of light,
And all life stretches for the sight
Again, of sunlight from its home,
From whence it to the earth has flown ;
For sun has parent love that draws
Us toward it—the attraction's cause ;
That law of parentage for their own
Is still in us for offspring shown ;
Inherent love that towards them draws
That mother love without a cause :
That toward her offspring cling if one
Should be disowned and all would shun ;
So sun-rays reaches all with love,
And draws all life toward her above.

DUAL LIFE.

EVERY thing we know is paired,
   Dual oneness is declared ;
The universe's attraction source
Is parent love—the central force ;
In its attractive force combined,
Are male and female—Dual Mind.
As the source from whence we came,
So is paired in us the same.
Two parts of every thing have we,

United product one will be ;
Two atoms in our body go
United, through its forces flow ;
Unite as one force equal powers,
In this small universe of ours ;
The male and female so combined.
Two atom lives unite in mind
Complete one electrical circle round,
In union only one is found ;
The positive and the negative one
Unite and personal become
One dual nature, acts from two parts ;
If in perfection we could start,
A perfect balanced power would be
And no sex superiority ;
And neither sex as marked be shown ;
If perfect balance both were grown.
All the universe is filled
With perfect love attraction still ;
That draws all systems round the one
Of Parent Love—its central sun.
The two in one of Dual Mind,
Within attractive force combined,
All Presence—God and Mother love,
Reaches all space and worlds above.
And atom lives in theirs express
This dual nature more or less ;
And parent love inherent move,
In us toward offspring, this doth prove ;
Binding all life in one embrace,
Of all there is in moving space.

THE ASSERTION OF SEX FORMS.

TWO atoms unite in the marriage of one ;
    As two lobes of the brain one mind will become,
Or two eyes that are normal blend into one sight,
So a positive and negative atom unite
In one electrical circle of motion ;
The one the most active in this mind commotion,
Asserts its predominence over the one
Less active in power, and the person become
The male or female, whichever it be,
That has the predominate power, you will see
Expressed in the sex of a person to grow ;
The union of which will heredity show.
And thus a dual nature have we,
The male and female has expression in thee ;
The right and left side of the body will show
Two things into one dual body will grow ;
Two atoms united in marriage of one ;
As two parts united one person become ;
So we in the progress of life motion see;
The course of progression to individualize thee,
In self-assertion the larger to grow,
And what your inherent atom life show,
For both so united each one will express
In the growth of each other their traits, more or less.
Two atoms united one person will be,
The positive and negative one are in thee ;
A body of many as one we will find,
In the growth of a plant all together combined ;

And yet an all-present personality will show,
In your consciousness, no part can sever, you know,
By the knife of the surgeon, your presence you feel,
Your identity somewhere, your person conceal ;
And so it continues, through waste of the years,
From youth unto age, when your youth disappears,
It is not the physical, but what it contains,—
The person of mind, that eternal remains,
In the image of God two powers are made one,
The male and female one person become.

ORIGIN OF THE MENTAL ATOM.

NATURE has many invisible forces ;
    Are they not all atomic, in all their vast courses ?
As all coarser substanses are atoms we see,
So of spirit atoms these forces may be,
Whose nature is action and electrical motion,
Have the nature invisible in mind commotion ;
Each atom of which is a unit of mind,
The force that arranges and strives to combine,
Its selections of matter in body and form,
That stirs it with motion and mind, to conform,
And is that invisible something to give
The clothing of matter, in which it doth live ;
Matter expresses a personal thing ;
And dissolves whenever life leaves it, again,
For life that rebuilt it as fast as decay,
Has left it to after dissolve all away.
And death, they proclaim, is the last of the mind,

Because 'tis unseen when it leaves the earth shrine.
Now, mind is unseen when it lives, moves and shows
Its expression in substance along which it grows ;
The substance so closely resembles its own,
That to move, it must move, and such it is known
As the body that lives ; why does it e'er cease
To move, think and act, and the mind-power release,
As long as 'tis organized, if it is that you say
That causes the mind, how is it, I pray ?
O, mind is that something that organized it ;
For as soon as mind leaves it no longer will get
New atoms to build it, as fast as decay
That wastes, and has left it, and then hear you say
That bodies make mind.   O, how can that be ?
For mind was that thing that attracts them you see,
That organizes substance, whatever the form,
And the life has the shape and makes it conform
To a body, and through it, the life is expressive,
Of striving to be either good or aggressive ;
No matter whatever that life is to be,
It moves, moulds that matter the shape that you see,
And when they have served all that life from them gains,
The motion that built it, goes out and remains
Bodies of matter, all motionless—dead,
Until they, too, separate,—parts each are fled,
But these atoms of matter progressed with life motion,
Feels the impulse more active of another commotion,
That life may a step higher, strive to reveal,
In materialized form—there itself to conceal ;
And wooed to a marriage two atoms unite,

In one dual being a little more bright ;
The strongest predominating, the sex it asserts,
From the one that is weakest the other subverts,
And either a male or female is seen,
Materialized up into life's moving stream ;
Moving onward to life that can think, love and feel,
Until the long chain of progression reveals.
Atoms material, making better conditions
For life in unfolding equal all its positions
That life is to take in fruition of mind,
That upward advances to each human kind ;
Yes, all that our bodies of matter possess,
Has been used o'er and o'er by minds of far less
Unfoldment than ours, in material form ;
But steps up the ladder of life now adorn
The beauty of mind in realized bliss,
In individual life-growth its first stage is this.
But we always have been in the atoms before,
And our primitive growth first began here to soar ;
To this stage it reaches when conscious of life ;
We think, love and feel, though it may be in strife,
For feeling our way out to heights we may reach,
We gather experience lessons that teach
Us wiser each day, until never more
Will our troubles be those we have met with before ;
And thus we arise from the thraldom of earth,
And darkness we meet in our primitive birth ;
Arise as the seed from the bosom of clay,
To blossom and fruit in the sun's warmer ray ;
Enrooted with earth like a tree in its flight,

Its life-course return to the root of this life,
As long as love draws them to dissipate strife ;
Return with the feeling to help those below,
To faster progress in the ways now they know ;
To shun many struggles they met on the way ;
So those that have waited for the life of to-day,
To start on their journey of living, to see
A light in the distance for posterity ;
So those that are waiting in archieves of time,
For conditions when they may begin life sublime ;
Will not be delayed by no chances before,
Because the material that's used o'er and o'er
Becomes better adapted for life to unfold
Now than ages before—those along ago old.
And those now far onward up the ladder of life,
Come back in their love to remove earthly strife,
That ignorance met in its primitive form,
When human began long before you were born.

THE ONENESS OF MIND.

IN what do you say does the mind power reveal?
   In consciousness that a body you feel ;
The surgeon may cut off your leg or your arm,
So much, then, of organization is gone ;
But you are still conscious your form is complete,
Mind is consciousness, is n't it ?—the life-giving seat
Of thought,—and that arm or limb you ever will feel ;
And no surgeon's knife its presence can steal
From your mind, as a unit its limit is one

Body complete, and will not become
Severed of any part of itself,
No matter where lies that invisible elf ;
It holds to some part of the body it made,
That which has ever its presence obeyed,
And will continue to move it, until it might hate
Every part of material, should it have a changed state ;
Then it leaves it all through, every part is bereft
Of motion, and life for the mind body left ;
But should it hold yet to some part of the form,
Its presence unseen may be there to perform ;
And it could command each part, though it be
Distant from it, through its law of affinity,
For mind power has love of attraction so strong,
Love over that, to which it did belong ;
Has something within it, of God like a thing
Of transmitting thought, through distance to cling,
A mesmeric force upon it declare,
When suddenly killed, its material there,
By the thought, it is mine, hold it yet still to move
With impressions, its last thought of action doth prove,
That makes it from danger strive to be free,
Involuntary impulse of thought still you see.
Our life has the brain as the seat of the mind,
If you hit it a blow will it yet be confined ?
O, yes, for affinity holds it still there,
But it closes in sleep, self-protecting with care ;
Unconscious it dwells, but 'tis held in the form
And all of its involuntary action goes on.

WHAT IS SLEEP?

WHAT is sleep, that it shuts itself up so enwrapt,
That mind in self-protection is apt?
It is that power mind holds to its primitive state,
A power that mind has from its youth to the end,
To return to the scenes and its youth life extend,
Return from the distance of age, though it be
Connected with time where it started to be ;
So mind in its sleep goes far down to the time
When it slept in the atom, secreted was mind
And that instinct still uses to make it secure,
In all the vast change that its living endure.

MIND NATURAL TO MOTION.

MIND shuts itself up in inclosure from thought
If by such a process self-protection is sought
So sleep is that primitive state of the mind,
That we carry still with us, as higher we climb,
Just as the mind carries its power to possess,
Every memory with it to age more or less.
If healthy the person he has it more clear ;
By disease of some kinds it might all disappear ;
And if it is fettered, inactive and dull,—
Held yet in the material,—or by a dent of the skull
The moment you raise it, and set the mind free,
It begins itself acting—you surely can see.
Held in material because there is yet,

In some parts of the body affinity yet,
And mind being single it cannot yet go
Until every part has released it, you know.
What is there but mind, that can stir, think and move,
Without being set in motion? To prove
That mind has that nature, if only set free,
To begin its own thinking—and awake it will be,
After it is unconscious, and held there so long,
It loses no part of itself in the form?
The form may be changed thrice over this while,
Independent it is and retains all it had ;
As soon as it sets up its thought-power again,
Everything that it knew you see it retain ;
So mind does not waste with the body and brain,
It commences to think—and its last thought will say ;
For it has lost nothing it had, while it slept,
While the body of matter constant changes has kept ;
But it couldn't waste any part of the mind,
For it closed itself up and in sleep was confined ;
It can live independent of matter,—in thought,
Although it is closely in love with it wrought ;
But thanks to the Infinite of such is Him,
Mind can wake from the densest of sleep and begin
To think of itself, its electrical motion,
Is action—and natural to all mind emotion ;
Unchanging in nature, so we never can die
If in unconscious sleep our senses may lie,
For as soon as we leave the body that binds,
We arise to a life that is fairer for minds ;
Where the mind is set free to select as it will

And it conscious awakes in a life fairer still ;
Because in its action, has consciousness grown,
And all that it added, within it is shown ;
Exists there, a grown atom larger, to find
The realm where it was a life-atom of mind.
As a seed is a tree before it has grown,
Concealed up within it would never have known
The body and branches and leaves that would grow
Out of that seed from an atom we know ;
So we from an atom of mind have begun
And larger have grown in the light of the sun,
Until it lit up the depths of our being,
To self-individualize conscious of seeing ;
Beholding the universe, bathing in light,
That streamed in our mind and gave us our sight ;
Drew in by attraction the breath of the air
And this breathing motion gave consciousness where
We came in conditions with thought to begin,
With the Being we lived in that led up to Him.
Led out into light of a limitless day,
To blossom and fruit in our lives every way.
Thus higher the law of motion doth tend
To move ever on from beginning to end ;
That energy flowing through Nature, to be
Everywhere present, is Mind that we see
Of intelligent power, before we began
To develop a thought—manifested in man ;
Such a substance must be in the primeval source,
Or we could not give it expression of course ;
For something like mind no never could come,

Such thinking results—out of nothing begun ;
And units of mind be expressed we well know,
If it was not atomic—that mind power we see
In Nature as force—its atoms are we.

THE ALL-SOURCE.

THE Source increase? that could not be
     By growth of atom individuality.
Supposing all boundary of space
Would organization of God embrace ;
If the atoms of His mind
Enlarging, growing, should combine
As much from their surrounding motion
As compared to their increased proportion,
Would not the fountain be the same,
But differently proportioned bulk remain ?
To illustrate :   We will take
An egg, and all its contents make
Just the fullness of its whole
An atom in it of a soul,
When individualized into the chick,
It fills it, when it pecks and picks ;
For room it takes not any more
Than that within the egg before ;
So we no larger fill Unknown
Of Life—when we are larger grown ;
The elements combined will be
Within our individuality ;
And only differently proportioned,

THE LYRIC OF LIFE.

Would be the contents of "All Motion."
And if no boundary to space,
There's room enough to all embrace.
God does not sit upon a throne,
As kings and presidents are known,
Sometimes in anger—sometimes in love ;
" We in His body live and move."

REINCARNATION.

MATTER in all its varied scenes
    Of here and there in lives it screens,
With bodies, must be moved with thought
That other lives upon it wrought ;
Where matter must have been before,
It came for us to work it o'er.
Once we were an atom force,
In a material one, of course ;
We helped to form a body then,
Before in this one we had been.
If we have lived before in life
And witnessed much of joy and strife,
If in an atom we have been
In some material body—when
We formed a part of nerve and mind,
While we were with them so combined,
And acted in the brain of thought,
Of some old sage, that had enwrought
On us his mind, and made us do
The work as servants of his view ;

Those thoughts impressed us as a dower
In concert action, gave to our
Mentality, that would us thrill
In flesh, his biddings to fulfill ;
That we retained when he expelled
Us from his body, and was quelled
Our motion, to life-giving power,
That coursed us through his flesh each hour,
Then reincarnationists are we,
For atoms made bodies before me.
If we the atoms have composed
Something magnetic, among those
That did make up ethereal form,
Or nerve force, long ere we were born.
For mind and matter must unite,
And matter must be yielding quite
Unto the mind, if it obey ;
And could it do it—think, I say,
If it could do what mind would tell,
Unless it understood it well.
Along its courses to transmit
A thought unto the brain, could it?
The atoms making up the nerve
Must catch the thought to do and serve ;
And if it had received that thought
In concert with the others wrought.
This must be reason sometimes, thrills
Respond, that all our being fills,
Respond unto a wave of thought,
That in our thinking is outwrought.

Though wonderous very it must be,
Nerve atoms must understand, you see,
To carry hurts unto the mind,
The thought of pain when burned we find ;
If it obey the thought and will
Of sentiments the body fill.
And somehow may we not recall
From that primeval life through all,
Somewhere before, where we have been.
Just as the atom will extend
Its sleep to older age of life ?
And may recall some scene of strife,
Or intense joy, in days of yore—
The atom life we were before.
Enclosed in sleep, mind dangers shun
When it unconscious does become,
To fall in sleep as do the flowers,
And close up all their waking powers.
Mind is a labyrinth most strange,
In all its varied growth and change.
And if our atom mind had been
Incarnate in the brain of men,
That lived a thousand years before
We might live somehow that scene o'er ;
Whose mind had thrilled the nervous frame,
That you composed within his brain ;
And thus its recollection wrought
Within you, in your after-thought
Of growing individual life ;
Some by-gone scene of distant strife,

Before you grew in all your powers,
To bud and bloom in mindful hours.
You held it as a seed might hold,
Some autumn scene of sunset gold,
That touched the tree from whence it fell,
Within the seed—the life it held ;
Some tale the zephyrs may have kissed
In blossom, ere in fold and twist,
It wrapt the seed, that it might grow,
Before it fell to earth below ;
Before it burst its prison shell
And showed a tree wrapt in its cell ;
That larger expanded out, and grew,
And clothed itself from air and dew ;
And showed a larger tree to grow,
Concealed so small in seed below
From which it sprung. So we may hold
Within our atom life—untold
Some scene, before where we had grown
And coursed in substance nerve or bone,
Imparted to our atom life,
Some thrilling scene of man or wife,
Wherein we moved and formed a part
Of atoms in the pulsing heart.
And when in after scenes we grew
To larger life our atom view,
Might not express in memory powers,
Reflections from primeval hours,
Because the brighter life we gain
Eclipsed in shadow to remain

Impressions on them made before,
That atoms gain repeated o'er.
And matter must progress this way
To better serve and thought obey.
To make conditions for a mind
To freely grow, and not confine
The mind-growth, as in primal days,
When it was fettered, but in ways
Of coarsest thought realms to unfold,
Some parts would grow, and others hold
Back, from expression in the form,
And make it inharmonious born.

PHYSIOGNOMY READS ARIGHT.

GROW out in some direction where
    Matter moved most ready, there
It had enormous growth expressed
Of mind, and ugly and distressed,
Were forms to look upon—from where
We stand to-day, and growths compare;
There cramped into some hideous shape
That took a long time to escape.
Through progression of matter, time
Has made material more with mind
To grow in all its equal powers;
And thus have bodies more like ours.
Matter affinitized more with life,
Expresses now beyond such strife,

Of forms and shapes, as when began
Material, long ago with man.
To clothe the atom-mind in growth,
Of individual form and worth
Of all that atom must contain.

PROGRESSION OF MATTER.

MATTER expresses now more the
   Conditions, that mind can draw and hold
It in all concert action when
Revealed, is seen the form of men;
Matter in concert will allow
Life beauty well developed now ;
For matter does not mind contract,
But concert with it matter acts ;
More full and round it shapes the brain,
And intellect is just the same.
Affinitized with thought will be,
Each organ well expressed—you see ;
Because material more or less,
With mind has heretofore progressed ;
The more 'tis moved to mind commotion,
More sensitive grows to thought emotion ;
Each life before had some extreme
Of character, where it is seen
With power sufficient there to move
Matter by extreme of love ;
And so in time matter is made

To yield to almost all thought grade
In life below us, to express
All kinds of traits the more or less ;
If by intense growth matter thrills,
Then for that trait matter fills,
And yields to mind in quick respond,
When touched by mind—some higher bond.
Matter progresses in this way
To yield to minds developed sway ;
When all the organs shall be full,
It finds matter that will feel its pull ;
Thus every trait of mind can show,
Progressed from extreme traits—below ;
The deer has mind extreme in fear,
The tiny feet to run is here ;
The lion selfishness in power,
And jaws would grow to best devour.
Its strength was in this trait of mind
Because the others were confined.
And so each life below, expressed
How materials, for each trait progressed
To culminate in form of mind
Expressed in man—more ballanced find
Each trait of character, so round,
More perfect shape the head is found ;
And as the fullness of our mind
Selects and doth such matter find,
To move harmonious to its will,
A perfect roundness all doth fill,
In every part of shape and form,

That doth an intellect adorn;
That is the height of human mind,
And faster upward now we climb;
For matter fills the air and spaces,
With atoms for the different graces,
To find unfoldment at the will
Of that strange thing that does it fill,
With life and beauty to ascend,
Towards progression's higher end;
And why we see on earth to-day,
More perfect forms in every way;
Because in that primeval time
The action most with human mind,
And beast, was self-protective thought;
And its extreme of action wrought,
A body having means to kill,
That would subserve its inward will,
That moved materials to unite
In all the different shapes of fright;
And mind was motion and would go
If bound, in ways that it would grow;
And mind was tenant thus imprisoned,
Until matter had thus arisen
Through species, each filled some full pleasure
In life's-full octave's onward measure;
More perfect shape of physic form,
Because the mind that does conform
It, with its motions can express,
Its fullness rounded out—and less
Of growth the baser, on to build,

In harmonious action of the will.
The selfish must life growth express
To gain survival with the rest;
The base with the soprano tone,
Perfects the mind when higher grown;
So all can blend as in a tune,
And thoughts of melody assume;
The base with all the rest is sweet,
If every organ can repeat
Its tone, then harmony is wrought
Out of the full growth of all thought;
Thus higher life growth is made known,
In thought, when each organ has its own
Assertion, in the human frame,
And material cramps it not the same
As in the long ago of time;
The form and face is shaped by mind;
And if matter has less yielding power
With mind, and moves not by its thought,
Then it must o'er and o'er be wrought,
Below the plane of human life;
Develop through the growing strife
Of forms, until it can unfold,
So life below us we behold
In different species having will
Expressed in shapes to flee, or kill;
For self protection is the thought
On which existence base is wrought;
The primal step of mind to gain
Assertion on the earthly plane;

The first condition which we see
Of growth in individuality;
For clothed with matter life is enshrined
Secure for growth of human mind.
'Tis plainly seen 'tis life's intent—
Security—where'er it went,
Its active nature held we know
From moving, would itself then grow.

USEFULNESS OF MATERIAL.

HELD by material substance around,
   Then its activity was bound.
So inert conditions it must gain
And why material forms ?—why explain
The atom life its selfhood found,
When by conditions it was bound.
So higher thought than ours will beam
In life's progressive moving stream;
Intelligence of higher power
Of life, in laws enabling our
Materials, new thought still to find—
Expression from an atom mind.

MATERIALISM.

OBJECTORS say materials make,
   The mind,—Then how could you become
Different from another one
That with you breathed the self same air,
Alike your food and not compare

In species—both be just alike,—
But different minds as day and night.
Side by side two plants may grow,
And each selects its own to blow;
Its life's identity is there
Within the seed—as atoms are
Each, selecting from the same;
Shows different life the seed contain,
And its identity is shown,
When each bursts forth and larger grown;
And so it is with life that you
Hold in identity as true;
If bodies make the human mind,
Self same conditions you would find,
Would make two persons just alike;
But each appropriate and make
In each a very different shape,
So mind made you and was the force
The atom held in it, of course,
The mental atom—growing mind—
With all its added powers combined;
As it unfolded more and more,
From what it ever was before;
But showed from whence that atom came,
By its identity the same;
True to its source—but formed to be
What the conditions gave to thee,
To well express inherent powers.
And this is life and such is ours;
But life doth other forms unfold,
Of worlds,—will later on be told.

THE EVIDENCE THAT ATOMS EXIST.

AS person grows,—from germs were we
    Then smaller yet we once might be;
Until by microscope unseen;
Or invisible in nature been
An unseen force or like its nature—
The unseen life of every creature
A unit force would reason show
'Twas personal, if person grow
Out of its expansion more,
It must have been personal before
It began to grow at all;
And why the proof of atoms small
Composing substances; we know
From germ forms personal, doth grow;
This is a proof that atoms all
Are first, when larger grows from small.
As some materialists now deny,
For atoms no one can espy;
Some things we know by comprehensions
When unseen are their force dimensions.

MIND ATOMS.

IF God's mind is Energy seen everywhere
    In Nature, and mind with that Energy compare,
As substance invisible, then cannot mind be,
An atom of God's mind—of that Energy?

And if natural to be in mind units now—
In atoms of mind, O who can avow,
That it will not the same be natural ever,
And each as a unit of mind be forever?
And if 'tis mind magnetism flowing as life
Throughout every part in spaces so rife,
And it is expressed in atoms of mind,
It has correspondence to all that we find,
Composing all substance, that we know or see,
The course and the fine would they not the same be.
Invisible something is substance we know
For nothing,—in presence, would be or would show;
So if an invisible presence is there,
It must be a something for something is air;
And is not all something of atoms composed?
It must be the same for of atoms are those,
In substance we see—then why not the unseen
Much finer—be atoms with spaces between?
Of atoms we know the air is composed,
For water is air condensed, and arose
The water becomes the air once again:
And water drops, atoms unseen will proclaim,
As we look through the microscope there to behold
All the atoms so varied in shapes will unfold,
Just as all creation in God we might see,
As atoms of Him in creations that be;
And live in His body embracing the whole,
In which all therein, does His spirit control;
The "One and All Mind"—of which atoms are made,
Each unit a mind individual some grade;

His life flowing out in all energy;
Of that life each person must be—
That life as God's magnetism, might be expressed,
All embracing His body as ours and no less;
And so our magnetic energy see
Composed of mind atoms it surely must be.
But we have another oneness of mind
Of consciousness in us, undivided we find
In all our body in every part,
That is a unit of mind from the start.
That grows by expansion larger of mind,
(In learning continues that nature we find);
That attracts the atoms the body to build,
That is the personal shaping us still.
And magnetism is a substance entwined,
A spirit substance similar to mind,
Made up of spirit atoms enshrined
With the material atoms—the force
In every atom, its center of course,
That is perceptible to the mind power;
That is searching in love for its atoms each hour,
Which it can touch with sensation of mind
And move the ethereal within them combined
In material cells, concealing that force
That must be the mind atom in it of course.
And so if attracting a body material,
It must from this reason have one—too ethereal,
Made up of spirit atoms unseen—
The spiritual body connecting between
Matter and mind;

And is the magnetic substance possessed;
By which we are known—and cannot divest
Of its coarseness, or fineness, unless with our mind,
It has an attraction, for that more refined;
And if for the love of the wise and the good,
Our mind seems to be, such can be understood,   .
By this atmosphere that will surely surround,
Filled with atoms progressed in quality, found
To be like ourselves, and of atoms composed
That inward and outward eternally flows.
For mind has its love for those atoms that draw
Toward it, combined in selections, its law
That in affinity to them incline,
And the atmosphere 'round them resemble the mind;
Aud others will feel their aura of light
Or otherwise darkness—their primitive night;
And sensitives will feel in this way the mind,
That a body doth hold within it enshrined;
If it hath correspondence with yours, you will feel
The power and the goodness they cannot conceal;
And both will the other in thought understand,
Through the windows of soul, or clasp of the hand;
But living will bring every soul into light,
Of love and of beauty to chase away night,
For night cannot always with darkness, enshrine
The growth of the soul, in the leap of the mind;
For out of the darkness it rises to-day,
And climbs ever upward in brightness alway;
Unfolding the blossom of thought in the soul,
All it has there inherent, in beauty unroll,

Unroll through the ages of time yet to be,
As branches and leaves and flowers on a tree
Speaks to the world its beauty and kind;
So we will be one of all human mind,
To show the ascendant of mind to progress
Out of all our selections from God's loveliness;
For everything here surrounds us we know
That will everywhere the higher we grow.

PROGRESS.

IF we can select it by growing supreme,
   And from this unknowable gather and glean
As electricians have gathered from out the same air
That which produces a light from darkness once there
To the ancients, that lived in the time long ago;
So we can yet gather more brightness, we know,
That is undiscovered by wisdom to-day;
Out of God, that surrounds us, in just the same way.
If we do not select what will give us a light
Out of the elements, then we have the night;
So in all the dark worlds, that is told of above,
God does not make them—everywhere is His love;
But ignorance yet, in the growth of the mind,
May be swept away and a light they will find,
That will banish in God these dark worlds, to bliss,
And if so, 'twill do it, the same here in this
World—for if death cannot send any wicked ones there,
But what in the mind growth is brilliant and fair,

Then no shadows above will shadow us here,
And all will ascend to a far brighter sphere
When they leave the earth life, to higher arise
In the marching of progress to life in the skies;
For God is all goodness, in which we all live,
And to all human longings its answers will give,
If we will but search for the wisdom of mind,
And through its own genius of living will find
The yet wondrous things of God that surround
Us everywhere, and it can be found,
What will bring us more glories as light has been known
And gathered from air as electric has shone.

THINGS OF SPACE.

SO that which gives the greatness to mind
     And joys of living, we yet, too, may find;
So God everywhere present will be,
Making heaven for us—which we cannot now see;
If we can discover what more can be there,
Besides what we now have found in the air,
The elements which combined to produce
What may be enraptures—as well as for use;
We now have discovered that different parts
Of elements mingled have different arts.
The sun rays in photographing is shown
The reproduction of us, that once was unknown;
As varied ever more elements are,
Could we but combine them would sparkle a star,

E

Of glory to us unthought of, unknown,
More luxuries ever than a King on a throne,
Might be our endownment if we could but find
From the elements round us, just those to combine,
These effects to produce, our wisdom must rise,
To bring its rich wealth as to those in the skies,
For Nature is everywhere equal the same,
If we can but find what its product will gain.

SPACE IS EVERYWHERE ALIKE.

THE planets that sweep through the spaces afar,
    The earth just the same as the most brilliant star,
Finds everywhere through the great distant fields
It speeds in its orbit the same Nature reveals
Life elements for health and fitted to breathe,
Or else through some spaces that from air would leave,
That gives the life substance contained in the air;
So Nature must have it alike everywhere,
To fill this life element found in the air.
Throughout the all distance of space as we roam,
So much is alike we feel it our home;
The elements of life combined must be there,
No matter what region in distance we are,
The same must be all the vast regions of space,
Or else in the orbit of earth we would trace
Some different substance comprising our air,
And this must be proof 'tis alike everywhere

In Nature and God, but differently proportioned for
    mind.
Progression will from it elements find
Out what, when united, will glory unfold,
And brightness of systems and worlds will unroll;
And from those bright worlds where the progress of
    mind
Has arisen in knowledge, for centuries find
The bliss which they tell of—when back they return
To earth, where their life first started a germ;
The tranquil and peace of those regions of bliss
That find no comparison to it—in this
Pristine condition, where mind on the tree
Of life is but fruit, that is green now, to be
Growing and living, until it shall find
The ripened perfection of all human kind.
If bitter and evil our life seems to-day,
By simply existing and living it may
Outgrow all the evil, and ripened will find
The joy of existence, for each human mind
In the glory and sunshine that God doth create,
It will ripen creation all sooner or late,
For ultimate being is flowing forever,
Designings for good, from the Glorious Giver.

THE AIR.

THE sweetest music ever known
    Was product of the air in tone;
To so combine the notes, that swells
Of air rushed through them, so compels

The unity of those combined
With harmonies—so is the mind
An instrument with notes combined,
That as we breathe the air we find
The life converts it into tone,
The voice of thought through it is known;
Converts the action through the mind
Of many organs so entwined,
That in the unity of tone,
The thoughts produced—each have their own
Harmonious action sweet and full
Of melody in spoken word,
Or discord, as the sound is heard;
That each one's mind in voice produce
By what the air contains for use;
'Tis not the air that each inhale
That tells for each a different tale,
The air they breathe is surely right,
Has all the properties alike;
But each life has a different mind,
Of organs active so combined
That life propelling—breathing air,
Make thoughts in some minds sweet and fair,
That have each organ full in tone;
While others lacking—some ungrown
Do so unite in active thought,
That discord is the sound outwrought,
Out of the life force, so combined
That some may have an evil mind;
What is the remedy?   Not the air

That both inhale so sweet and fair,
That both are breathing it, the same,
The instrument is all to blame,
Through which the life concerts to be
The product of thought minstrelsy.
The remedy would be to reach,
To every human mind and teach
Them how to make each organ full
In growth, and discipline, to school
The growing strength of mind each hour
That every organ have full power.
And then no evil there would be
But different genius of mind, see
The action will in both produce,
The melody for different use.

THOUGHT IMPROVEMENT.

THAT each in the creation given
     Have varied hues of thought for heaven;
That like the choicest flowers will be
Perfection different to see;
Each sending forth the sweet perfume
Of thoughts select, like choicest bloom.
Or like the harmonies of sound
That notes produce in music round
In sweetest melodies of tone;—
Music of mind thoughts each their own,
So justly made to perfect blend
In onward being without end.

And all discordant minds will be
Things of the past,—no evil see
Because through mind as it has grown
Into perfection each their own
Identity in future life,
Has found that peace beyond all strife,
That all are seeking so to gain;
The constant draw that will attain;
Which is the purpose and the end
That all our lives toward, extend;
That is progression's constant law
Towards a higher life to draw;
This Energy that moves the air
And all in space and everywhere;
Because the ultimate and end
Throughout, to every thing extend,
By growth into perfecton's flower,—
A fulness of inherent power,
That must proceed with moving time,
The nature of All-Seeing Mind
Is time and distance without end
In circling rhythms to extend.
And light of mind in future days,
May so invent in genius ways,
May so construct the keyboard sound,
Through echoes so enclosed around,
That it will harmonize in tone
In concert, to produce unknown
Melodious strains, with this same air
That nothing with it can compare,

Or is produced by it to-day,
In softest, sweetest, music strains,
While all the air as now remains;
But out of its effects may see
Produced that which shows that there may be
Within this instrument of mind,
Something new that may unbind;
For mind growth hath eternal powers,
And will develop as it towers
To heights supreme, in something new,
And then the elements we view
To-day around us, may disclose
The beautiful, beyond all those
Effects that e'er before was seen
And not as much of God will screen,
In the invisible display,
Of what the air contains to-day,
But will rejoice by what we know
The air contains while here below,
For us to gather and unite
Besides the element of light,
That has been found within this age,
Until they solved the question quite
That came forth in electric light,
The coarsest element in air
That is invisible everywhere;
Which first in strivings we have touched,
And we have found this helped us much;
So we more beauteous things will find
In onward searchings for the mind;

Producing ecstasies of bliss
And making joys of heaven in this
World, which has the air around,
Containing all that has been found,
In any heaven far above
Existing in supremest love;
Because the mind has grown to see
And to discover what may be
Within the elements of God;
That fills all spaces ever trod
By angel feet or great mind powers.

MORE OF THE AIR.

WHERE do the colors of the flowers
That they instinctively do trace
From Nature's secret hiding place,
In feeling out for and selects,
That which its loveliness protects,
As well as all the blossom sweets,
Their life from out the air completes;
For this the orchid flower explains,
That always in the air remains;
All its beauty comes from there,
It all is found within the air;
That which it draws to form the leaves
And stem and flowers—its life perceives;
And reaches by the thought of love,
And builds it, one, on one, above,

Until it has a form complete,
And shows what it has found so sweet,
Out of the atoms found in air,
Its life selected everywhere;
Out of the air to form the flower
When moved by its life giving power.
The air contains all we behold,
And much and more ten thousand fold,
It holds in its solution rare,
Unknown to us, we call it air,
As if that did it well express,
In finding more or something less.
You say it gets it from the sun
Its beauteous colors every one.
Then doth the rainbow get its hues ?
With air vibrations as some views
Have been advanced, if it were so
The air is filled with this we know,
Is filled with all the colors fine
That e'er can be, or may combine
In the expression of a flower;
And mingle with the richest dower
Of all the air is said to be
That is unknown to you or me.
The air holds all there is in space,
Or we a difference could trace
In the components of its parts;
As earth in revolution starts
And sweeps the distant boundaries where
There would be change within our air;

If something different should unite
With it, to change its nature quite.
It loses nothing we can see
Or gains for life, so it must be,
It finds in all the distant fields
Of spaces wherein its orbit wheels,
The same existing life, to fill
The atmosphere, with forces still,
The same as what it had before
It went its orbit o'er and o'er;
Our atmosphere would lose or gain
Unless through space, all was the same,
Filled with life giving forces where
It kept supplied our atmosphere
With elements of life to gain,
And air kept filled with life the same;
But differently it well may be
Proportioned in what we could see,
Outside of the surrounding air,
That earth had for her atmosphere.
That earth attracts like living things,
What her selections to her brings;
And reaches out as doth the flowers,
In life exhibiting their powers,
To draw and to select their own;
That which it loves—a life is known,
To build up different forms to be
Expressed in different shapes, we see
Of life, that all creation fills,
Expressing each their different wills;

Their needs, they find within the air
From all combined within it there;

The germ, that shape and form unfold
Within the earth, the air must hold,
For up it troops into the light
And gathers from the air, the right
Of what it needs, to thus express
Its leaves and flowers of loveliness.

THE FIRST DEVELOPMENT OF LIFE ON PLANETS. ·

THE new fresh earth turned to the air,
    Is kissed by dews that fall from there;
And elements in rays of sun
And rain, before a growth begun.
And new forms rise, no seed is sown
Unless from air its germ has flown,
Into the earth, that kissed by sun
And dew and rain its life begun;
We know the raindrop fell from air,
Has many life germs in it there,
When with the microscope we see
The millions of variety;
And if life gathers for its need
Out of the air when burst, from seed,
Then air must be its native home.
And have all in it which has grown
Upon that form to clothe its need
Besides the germ within the seed;

Then air must everywhere enfold
The elements that bodies hold;
Which they in changing growth expel,
And new materials draw as well.
And in new Islands of the sea
Could life thus spring up first to be ?
Some coral island far from view,
In mid-seas with life creatures new ?
That must have sprung to being there
Out of the kisses of the air,
That touched those island lands so free ?
That coral builders of the sea,
Assisted by the mud and shells
Packed into them by ocean swells,
Had made with all their beauty rare,
Land, trees, and flowers, not anywhere,
But where enrooted they had sprung
Up into being new and young ?
Did those life germs come from the air
And elements in earth repair ?
Or those germs of all life, come
From the sun rays new begun
All that atoms held within
As conditions to outbring ?
All the species found are there
Come from life germs in the air
As conditions of their love
Reaching it from life above ?
Did they in the dewdrop fall
Or the raindrop have germs of all

That upon that island rested,
In its virgin sôil,—divested
Of all seed that could be sown
Or from other lands have blown ?
Such the air contains we know
Germs of all things here below;
For they rise in air and mist
From the forms that do exist;
Vegetable or animal,
Fills the air, all they contain
From their bodies, thoughts and brain.
Atom germs they all express
Are exhaled, for new are dressed.
Constantly every hour in living,
To surroundings we are giving,
We are knowing, or the rose
From the seed could not disclose,
All that atom rose contained;
As it swelled with sun and rain,
To a larger rose tree there
Clothed with beauty from the air,
Stem and leaf, then bud and flower
By the life within of power;
Moving it to thus disclose
The invisible the rose,
By its garments atom made
That within the air had stayed,
Until its beauty so supreme,
From the air did pick and gleam

Atoms, that the body made
And the physical displayed,
By the clothing that it drew,
Brought the invisible to view.
So with every other grade
Of life, that has existance made;
Every creature that has been
From the lowest up to men;
For one law for all must be
In the growth of all we see;
Modes are used to bring about
God's expressive meanings out;
And the wondrous air must hold
All there has been new or old;
By developements extreme
In some thought directions seen.
Some imperfect growth has found
In material to disclose
Consciousness, was life's purpose,—
That in time it would attain
Through its pleasure and its pain,
All that living for us gain,
In the purpose of its life,
Rising out of growth and strife,
That the pristine growth would be
Strugglings for identity.
And the selfishness must grow
To survive its life we know;
So upon the lowest plane
Life its first expressions gain;

Selfish forms, thus first were seen
Growing out in great extreme.
Isles that life growth first was winning
To its bosom life's beginning.
God is present everywhere
In the earth, the sea and air;
So from God all life was made,
Through conditions every grade;
And from Him our life doth draw,
Through the life growth and its law;
For is God not everywhere
In the spaces and the air?
Where the elements doth hold
All the life germs that unfold?
How wondrous then must be the air,
Even the frost work everywhere
Imprinted where its touch is made
Shapes in forms of every grade
As they naturally combine,
Again in shape they did entwine.
For air congealed, shows leaves and flowers,
And trees and lands and city towers,
In which materials have been made
That the mind thought has displayed.
Leaving it to crumble—where
All becomes again the air,
Shapes in air resemble us—
Photographs, or mirrors must
Demonstrate this fact to be,
Moved by light so us you see.

It is not us—but it is then
The forms of us that doth extend
By marvelous power contained in light;
Light is in the air so bright
To reproduce ourselves again,
And picture o'er where we have been;
All this is wondrous power of air,
What is within it everywhere.
And may be we can read again,
Upon this book of Nature when
We clearer see with spirit eyes,
What will us very much surprise;
What is reflected on the night,
May be revealed again by light;
The silvery fore-ground doth reveal
Our mirrored self, that doth conceal
In Nature, only as we go
Before the mirror glass, we know.
And so upon deep Nature's night,
All may reveal within its light.
What we have been, or were before,
May be repeated o'er and o'er,
In the vibrations of all time,
Throughout all worlds to the sublime.
So let us live if this is known,
So we can feel to claim our own;
And know we lived the best we knew
In this far reaching pristine view.
If we should meet it may it tell
We lived our best, and lived it well.

If nothing can be ever lost,
These life scenes we again may cross;
If everything reflects in space,
All things may thus have room and place,
And in the elements combine
As fruits of our primeval mind.
If thoughts are things they help to build
Our book of life with pages filled;
This book of Nature that may throw,
The mirage of our life below
Upon the camera of time,
And if the good the bad outshine,
This darkened background may help show
Our better deeds with shining glow;
And so the picture may be given,
Of life work better seen in heaven.
But let it be so that the night
Of deeds, may be obscured by light,
That will reflect from good deeds done,
As night dispels from rays of sun.

COMPREHENSION OF TIME AND DISTANCE.

TWO cities might be miles apart
That from a certain point would start;
And reckoned so by that between
The two—the mile posts that were seen.
But were both cities blotted out,
And mile posts we should do without

The distance 'twixt them—still would lie,
That you had no way to espy.
So distance that we comprehend,
In space, would still itself extend
If every thing within it there,
Were blotted out—the worlds so fair;
Then distance is that something seen
Beside the worlds that come between;
That something by "All Presence" known,
The distance, space—within all grown;
Filled with attraction—its all source
And that is Love—attraction force.
There would be something we call time
From youth to that of age sublime;
A distance if no years had flown—
The marks by which the time is known;
By comprehension time is seen,
If years should never come between—
They are the periods of time,
Marks made by us, that we combine;
And so the distance of the spheres,—
The space between, we call the years;
The time that takes each one to go,
So much of space—we reckon so;
But time and distance would be still
If periods were not there to fill.
What is this time and distance there?
It is "All Presence" everywhere.
A something that we comprehend,
That farthest distances extend;

We only can this presence see
Of time and distance that must be,
By what we comprehend with mind
A something which we call the time;
But if no years were anywhere,
This presence-time would still be there;
The space and time it takes to go,
From one unto the other, so
If 'twas not marked by us or seen,
The distance would be there between.
All Presence—distance we will call,
Filled with all life throughout it all;
And its attractive moving force
Is Love—mind sentiment—and source
That " Ever Presence " seems to fill,
Revolving words around it still.
Is it parental love that draws
All things toward " All Seeing Cause ? "
For parent love binds all that live—
Inherent, we to offspring give.
This fills immensity with mind;
Love is attractive law to bind
All, in one universe, embrace;
Attraction filling every place;
And cause the one great moving force
That draws all systems round its Source.

WORLDS. THEIR CAUSE OF ORBIT MOTION.

SPACE is full of substance moving,
    Or distance would not space be proving;
A sun in space revolves around
And elements in which it turns
Move around the heat that central burns.
Then worlds within space will of course
Go around this same attractive force.
As whirlpools carry all around
The bodies that therein are found;
Thus they have orbits 'round the sun,—
A spirit or material one;
No matter what the force that draws,
An orbit motion it will cause,
With all the things that form in space
The small and great in every place;
Will in the elements go 'round
The central force as far as bound
By an attractive force, that draws,—
An orbit motion it will cause,
Of star dust, meteors, or asteroids,
All go around—there is no void;
All in moving motion, whirls
Around the sun within space,—worlds
Are going in their orbits too
With elements unseen to view.
As far as earth's attraction runs
She draws the moon—as does the suns

Around their revolution force
Upon their axis,—is the course,
That everything attraction draws,
Move around that force and is the cause
That those the nearest swifter move,
And slower farthest off will prove.

ELLIPTICAL ORBITS.

WHY worlds in elliptical orbits move,
    This law electrical* will prove;
Two worlds unequal you will see
In their electrical identity;
Toward the larger, one will draw,
In orbit line through this same law;
In perihelion—they become
Equally electrified as one;
They then repel and onward speed,
The one that sun, or earth, thus feed,
And on in orbit speeding yet
To apohelion—losing it;
Unequalized, thus as before,
Repeats its orbit o'er and o'er.
And thus the planets round the sun,
Elliptical, in orbits run;
Or moon around the earth will bring;
The same law moves in everything,

---

*"There is a principle in philosophy—That two balls unequally electrified, the stronger will attract the weaker towards it, when imparting their superabundence to the other, they become equally electrified they will again repel."—*Comstock's Standard Works.*

'Till assimilating they repel,—the cause,
Electrical attraction draws;
That positive and negative, must combine
To keep in union powers of mind;
For if both positives become,
Or both are negatives in one,
They will repel—'till losing it,
Will then draw towards, as opposites;
But if two mind-powers would unite
In harmony forever right,
They must be opposites of mind,
Natural in temperament all the time.
As male and female force become,
A dual atom—two in one.

FORMATION OF WORLD LIFE.

BY aggregation earth has grown,
　From the small meteoric stone,
The stone had elements complete,
Which would produce spontaneous heat;
Surrounded by the depths of earth,
The central force of planets birth,
Of motion,—when its central force
Created a revolution course;
What is the meteoric stone?
Its properties combined as known,
Are iron, sulpher, rock completing,
Moisture naturally secreting;

Experiments of " Prof. Lemier," *
In the sixteenth century year,
Upon what caused volcanoes—found,
That iron filings, sulphur, ground
And water, covered o'er with dirt,
Would spontaneous heat, itself convert.
The pressure of the world would grind
Its central properties combined
And moisture that the rocks secrete.
So from this center earth has grown
And buried the meteoric stone;
Which has those properties composed,
Of iron, sulphur, all of those,
That would spontaneous heat produce;
And central heat made by its use;
The heat would melt the mineral all
And form a central liquid ball;
From the specific gravity
More in minerals tend to be;
Which draw towards the center all
And forms a melted mineral ball;
And central heat—around will flow
The cooler particles we know;
And lava formed from melted stone
Outward toward the surface thrown.
At the equator, with the sun
Life growth, was there the first begun.

———

* " A scientist of the sixteenth century, a Frenchman. In his experiments searching after the cause that produced volcanoes, found that iron filings, and sulphur and moisture, covered with earth produced spontaneous heat."—*Laws of Heat.*

And polar electricity toward center draws
And meeting, more of heat would cause,
As two polars meet, to magnetism turns,
Like arc lights causes heat that burns,
And electricity's natural course,
Revolves around, a circular force.
Thus planets motion I am solving,
By its electricity revolving.
All these forces do combine,
That earth's revolving motion find;
Gives the life motion of a world,
When on its axis it is whirled.

ORBIT MOTION GATHERS ELECTRICITY.

ITS belt of orbit motion runs
    So swift in motion round the sun;
This motion generates thus from space,
Electricity from every place,
As the dynamo motion, where
It picks electricity from the air,
Its orbit is so swift through space
This motion attracts from every place;
This motion for its use would be
For motion gathers electricity.
And toward the planet comes this force
That equalizes this swift course
Unknown to us, we do not feel
The swift motion, that in orbits wheel;

A law so provident to us,
Motion so swift without it, must,
If moving contrary to the currents find
Our atmosphere streaming out behind;
As comets with their light will shine;
Attraction draws them toward the sun,
As meteors to the earth will come,
And whirling in magnetic stream
Around the sun, they come between
Us and the sun's electric light,
Within its atmosphere so bright.
And cause the spots we on it see
As transit of Venus seems to be;
They bring in elements of star—
The sun rays from those spaces far,
As water goes in mist,—and rain
Returns unto the earth again.
The lightning is a ball we know
If it were only moving slow,
It makes a hole just as a ball
Would pierce its way if seen at all.
If lightning electricity could be seen,
It would be round and not a stream.
What is a cyclone? could you see
Its center of electricity,
Then you would see the whirling force,
Of electricity's natural course.
As with the earth it whirls around
From polar to the center bound.
For electricity's natural course

Is 'round and 'round as axis force.
At positive poles, to central flows,
And meeting in magnetism that outward goes
Unto the surface, formed in heat,
And constantly this force repeat,
At the equator with the sun,
Which cause the growth there first begun.
For planets grew, as others grow,
From small to larger worlds we know;
From meteoric stones in space,
They grew to find a planet's place.
So far from other worlds they grow
That not attracted they will so
Assume their life, as larger grown,
That they can self protect their own.
We'll talk of this more by and by
But first we would the sun espy.

INFANT SUNS.

WHERE the electric substance fill
　　Spaces and distance as it will;
Bodies could be attracted there
As stones that fall from out our air
Begin from elements to combine
As meteors which we find,
Doth centralize in fields of air;
So gases would in spaces where
Suns began, and threw their light

Through all the fields of space so bright;
When they to larger bodies grew
For us to see their brightening view;
Begins to form electric—cold,
And all of energy they hold;
And as they larger do become,
The greater motion have each one;
By motion is attracted more,
Just as we told you heretofore
That electricity is found
And gathered, by swift motion 'round,
And larger 'round would they become
Until they grew to be a sun.
Revolving motion is the love
That electricity doth move,
And this around and 'round would whirl,
Upon an axis such a world,
That had itself an energy
Of substance like electricity,
And make for all electric light,
A sun in space shining so bright;
Suns would not grow when equal threw,
Its sunlight out, as fast as new
Electricity it did attract;
As their life motion now suns doth act;
Or after its limit growth it knew,
(As about twenty 'tis so with you;)
For suns are living bodies too,
Like every life, in me or you,
Or life that does not breathe, will grow,

And only the involuntary action show;
But when life breathing motion, more
Adds to its power not had before;
The voluntary then is seen
With the involuntary to gleam,—
In thought perception higher still,—
The animated life and will
Is manifested, as you see,
With air, and mind in chemistry;
The spiritual that the air contains,
Where oxygen in it remains.
Suns throw off their substance there,
Creating their illumined air;
The sun would cease its growth to make
After it gained illumined state;
For rays thrown off would equalize
The gathering process, otherwise;
It throws its rays in space afar,
To every planetary star;
And its magnetic central heat,
Created where the forces meet,
Are full of atoms,—forces made
Up of life germs of every grade,
Electrical those atoms are
That fill the sun-rays to earth-star,
Gone out of it in force of love,
That draws all life to sun above;
That starts on planets—hidden force
Of atom life,—the sun its source;
On the earth surface to create

Their first luxuriant growing state,
For bud and bloom must have the light
To perfect blossom, if it grows,
All true observers this well know.
And electricity is a thing,—
A substance unseen, to bring
Atoms in its composition,—
The force invisible for transition,
Of germs into the living forms,
That doth earth's surface so adorn;
These unit atoms central draw,
With energy, though called a law;
And such its nature in material;
A central force they hold ethereal;
And magnetism of the sun
Is kindred with us, every one;
It held us in pre-natal birth,
It is our parent—sun with earth.

THEIR LAW OF MOTION.

THE suns must form in distant space
　　When not attracted from their place,
Would larger grow to be a sun,
When its electric light begun
To shine in space, a world you see
Composed of electricity.
The north and south electric lode
Meet in the center and explode;

Creates the electric light that burns
Where electricity to magnetism turns;
Makes its illumined air of surrounding space
The great electric sun in space;
And its swift motion attracting more
From Mother Nature's surrounding store,
As fast as it expended light
Into far space—surrounding night,
'Tis central held by planet law
That in surrounding orbits draw;
And on an axis 'round would whirl
By the same law that turns a world.
Electricity, the polar force,
Circles 'round its natural course;
To magnetism in the center turns,
And heat-producing central burns.
And swifter far would turn a sun
Because 'twas spiritual begun;
It is an element of life,
And naught impedes its motion rife;
Electricity makes light in any place,
When generated in a ball,
As lightning shows unto us all
A light that represents the sun
And in a vacuum will become
A light, so 'tis its nature where
In space it burns without our air,
And gives a light as does our sun,
Which shows that electricity is one
Of the suns, properties begun;

As arc-light, where two polars meet
Doth the electric light complete;
An electric and magnetic ball,
As one into the other turns,
Creates the central heat that burns;
As it **throws off** its **substance** there,
Creating its illumined air;
The **sun** one **great** electric light,
Whose motion gathers it from night
Of space, **where** all is circling 'round,
Full of electric forces found.
Such is the body of the sun,
Instead of a material one.
In worlds of **energy** unseen,
Electric lights these spaces gleam;
'Tis only their illumined air
We **see** surrounding them so fair;
That to us shapes their bodies round,
As gas, **unseen, the** jets surround,
With light, **a distance** from **them the phase,**
Creating their illumined blaze.
Bodies could **be** attracted there,
As well as meteors **in our air,**
To larger grow, revolve and **act,**
If larger bodies do not attract
Them away from where they are,
They grow to be a sun or star;
The same in far-off spaces, where
The sun exists without our **air;**
And generates itself, you see,

As meteoric stones must be,
That have the property of earth,
And are a world of infant birth.
So infant suns may grow this way,
As balls of electricity to-day
That greater bodies to them draw,
As earth, in meteoric law;
The greater bodies lesser—(know)
Attract, and lesser cannot grow
To be a world or sun in space;
For all is filled and have their place,
But organization is a law
And worlds these lesser bodies draw;
As it is natural to combine
Elements in space we ever find;
From water drops that fall through space,
In feathery stars, this law will place
The particles to so combine;
And drops in miniature we find
Of worlds—as it a bubble floats
Out into space, this law promotes
Some shape, is forming through this law;
In balls, all drops of liquid draw;
Electric balls in space unite
With motion natural to light;
And larger grow to be a sun,
The same as a material one,
Will grow from meteors to be;
As asteroids your glasses see,
Have grown since " Jupiter " did show,

With telescope, itself, you know.
And so at first began a sun,
Revolving motion it begun
Because it is natural so to move,
Electric motions this doth prove;
And motion 'round attracted more,
Still growing larger than before;
Just with its rapid motion fed
Itself from space, which shows instead
Of wasting it increases more
By motion gathering as before
It is electricity we see
The substance feeding it to burn
That it attracts by axis turn;
And so it feeds itself to-day
With electricity the same way;
And why its body we can see
Is its surrounding light that we
Observe that ever shapes the sun,
And spots are bodies that have come
Between us and itself to screen
The light as they are often seen;
We call them spots upon the sun,
As Venus' transit seems to one,
So electricity is found
By motion of revolving round.
This motion is its natural law,
While heat and light in straight lines draw,
So outward toward the surface flows,
At the equator heat straight goes.

G

CONDITIONS FOR LIFE ON THE EARTH'S SURFACE.

A ND with direct rays of the sun
   The planets' surface there becomes
Fitted for life growth to appear,
Which thus attracts its atmosphere;
In life's selections reaching forth
To gather to it needed worth
That to the planet's body draw
Full of life germs a common law;
What growth expels the air is full
And for their needs they constant pull
Toward the planet out of space
And every thing their bodies grace;
But ere this stage of being grew
The planet's life, the water drew;
Reaching for elements of its kind,
Whose unity is water's freak,
And rocks this element secretes;
And moisture of the atmosphere,
Before life germs on earth were here;
Life forms that doth in water live,
These germs did to the planet give
The life forms first that water hold
So many varied and untold.
The germs that higher forms express
In self-growth to more loveliness;
What bodies need for their repair

The life of growth attracts them there;
And so the space around the world
Is full of what its growth unfurls.
All bodies thus have atmosphere
Containing what their life and sphere
Attracts to them,—what they expel,
Or draw to them, surroundings tell;
And so a world attracts around
Life germs, all substance on it found;
And this is full, as doth appear,
Unorganized, in atmosphere.

ATMOSPHERE PRODUCES HEAT.

WHERE growth is most prolific, there
It has a greater, deeper air,
And heat produces from the sun,
As valleys full of growth become;
While on the mountain top is snow,
The air is thinner there, we know.
This law applies to every one
Of planets, moving 'round the sun,
At Mercury, nearest sun, the air is thin
Around the planet, to begin;
And deeper grows around each one;
The farther distant they become;
This law gives heat to all alike,
So beautiful it is and right.

HEAT AND LIGHT ON ALL WORLDS.

"NATURE," so provident for need,
    Cares so protecting for her seed;
And growth increases air around;
Proportioned to the distance found
From sun, and all get heat as you,
And light, and sun, and air, and dew.
As well protected is the one
That moves the nearest to the sun,
Whose atmosphere is thin and rare,
So heat would not as much be there,
As those in distant spaces where
Their growth makes deeper atmosphere,
Get as much light and heat as here;
The sun-glass demonstrates this law,
The focused rays more light will draw,
So atmosphere encircling 'round;
The laws of growth have made profound;
To give all worlds their heat and light;
Their atmosphere to make this right,
And thus our praises will arise
To God, in this new thought surprise.
You know a law of life is there,
All present pulsing everywhere,
That atmosphere, combined with sun,
Proportions heat on every one;
And worlds the nearest suns are found
With atmosphere the least around;

And those the farthest, having more,
Combines more heat as told before.
In valleys greater heat is there
Than heights where atmosphere is rare;
This law gives heat on everyone,
Compared to depths of air, with sun.

MORE ABOUT ORBITS AND WORLDS.

THE atmosphere around the world
    Is moving with his axis whirl;
And out in space doth also draw
As far as its attraction law;
The elements move 'round the world,
And bodies in it 'round are whirled;
By this the moon doth 'round earth draw,
In orbit of revolving law,
But being so very far away
She moves it slowly in this way,
But earth's attraction must there go,
To make the tides that ebb and flow;
As far as earth's attraction goes
The elements around it flows.
This makes the orbits of each one,
The moon and planets, 'round the sun.
For space is full there is no void
From star, to sun, and asteroid.
It has a different proportion,
Of some things near the planets motion;

Because the atoms gather there
That growth attracts within the air;
More of material in proportion
Than far away from planets motion;
More for material growth we find
Mingled with that which feeds the mind;
Beyond this atmosphere are uses
Of elements that mind produces;
That feeds the mind with quicker thought,
Than mind and matter both enwrought;
That are the properties of air;
You know there are invisible forces,
That feed the mind, in air it courses.
The oxygen deprived from air
Or something associated with it there
Unconscious, we at once become;
So spirit feeds the mind, each one—
And outside of this air we know,
Such spirit forces surely flow,
That our life motion will inhale
When we have left material veil.

ATMOSPHERIC LAW.

DIRECT rays of sun with air
   On the earth's surface mingling there,
Produces heat upon the earth
And light in properties of worth.

Atoms attract from out all space
Toward a central force or place,
That does in love those atoms draw
And this is atmospheric law;
As they this loving impulse feel,
A hidden force they do reveal.
Space is filled around the earth,
With atoms that on it have birth;
This deepens where the most doth grow
As 'round the torrid zone we know;
The waste of all material mould
Where atoms new replace the old,
Make atmosphere around it more,
Than what had been there before.
That reaches out for what it needs,
And all life growth upon air feeds;
Thus air from space to earth is bound
A similar substance moving 'round,
With planet motion, through the love
That life growth has for that above;
Differently proportioned as to place—
More atoms than outside in space;—
Atoms of the material kind
Which is the atmosphere combined,
Producing cold, where it is rare,
And heat where thicker is the air;
As on the mountain top is snow,
And flowers and fruit in vales, below,
Gradating towards the temperate zone,
Where so much lesser life has grown;

And fla tened at the poles is seen
The earth, in shape, from this I glean.

WHY THE EARTH IS FLATTENED AT THE POLES.

A knowledge from this fact to show,
    The worlds where life upon them grow;
Is builded larger round the zone,
Where great luxuriant life has grown;
And nothing grown around the poles
The earth or world would flattened be,
In that locality, you see;
In building up ten thousand years
Of time, and growing of the spheres;
Nearer the equator everywhere;
The earth grows faster, larger there;
For it attracts so much from space,—
Its luxuriant growth repeating, place
So much upon its surface there,
That earth grows faster larger there.

WHY THE MOON IS NOT AN OLD PLANET.

A world cannot be old and dead,
    Unless it had this shape instead
Of round, as what we see the moon;—
An infant world not yet in bloom;

In shape the moon is seen to be;
Instead of old and dead to thee;
For 'twould be flattened at the poles,
If 'twas a world that had grown old;
From this we reason, where growth had been
Depression at the poles,—is then;
But it has not commenced to draw
To it much atmosphere—Growth law,
And growth if any cannot be
Where atmosphere is thin you see
Except in water germs may there
Be growing for they need not air,
Oxygen and hydrogen gas unite
And turn to water sparkling bright,
And form constituents of air,
Around the planets surface rare.

WORLD MOTION GATHERS ELECTRICITY.

THE dynamo of electric power
   Sets wheels in motion in the air
And electricity gathers there.
So the results of planet motion,
Swift in their orbits of commotion,
Draws the electricity from space
And cause their motion which we trace;
That planets are moving swift in space,
In belt of orbit as we place
The distance so extreme to go
In every minute's time we know

Would attract from out the spaces
Electricity, and all the phases
Of its axis motion, then
Revolve around as it has been
Doing, by a cause unknown,
Ere this reason it were shown;
Why upon their axes 'round
Worlds are turning it is found
That electricity has this motion,
And will produce just this commotion,
In planetary systems where
It fills all moving bodies there.
The polar electricity's will meet,
And in the center create heat;
They soon revolve, begin to turn,
When heat within their center burn.
Asteroids revolve we see,
Their orbits swift attract as we;
As electric to magnetic turn,
The heat is made to central burn;
And elements within it there,
Spontaneous heat makes lava there
Revolve around the cooler parts
As liquids, when heat motion starts;
Revolve around the central heat,
That air or liquids will complete.
And nothing resists the planets turn,
Suspended in space as we can learn.
So causes, thus turn 'round a world,
That on an axis starts to whirl;

With its life motion so complete
Continuing on to more repeat.
And the material there within
Unites in melted ore so thin
Its substance flows like water 'round
Where central heat to lava melts.
The poles are positive, cold is there,
But turns to heat in center where,
From the center outward flows,
The heat unto the surface goes,
At the equator all around
And surface heat was first thus found.
Central heat was first created
With these different powers related;
Combined with elements unknown
Found in the meteoric stone,
Where first its infant life begun,
For planets grow this way each one.
Those elements now have their use
Spontaneous heat to more produce;
To make a living body when
It larger grew and life extend.
The north and south electric lode
Meet in the center and explode,
Because repellent are their motion
And heat results from this commotion
Within the growing planet, where
Their surface growth attracts the air.
And electricity toward earth draws
From the orbit motion, cause

This force toward the planet, hold
All that around the earth enfold.
If sun is kindred to the earth,
In direct rays to give the birth
Of germ life, that its rays doth hold,
And 'round the torrid zone enfold;
To leap from Nature's hiding places,
Up into air and life's sweet graces,
In pristine earth's unfoldment shown
Where great luxurient life is grown;
Does not the earth its polar draw
From the north star through love and law?
Electricity so cold,
That makes it positive at the pole;
Direct in course from north it comes
From polar star so there becomes
Sometimes the brilliant northern lights,
Producing phenomena and sights,
That electricity is known
To be the same at frigid zone;
And with the earth this positive pole
Influences motion circling 'round
The course that electricity is bound,
And also magnetism thus turns;
And both these motions well affirm,
Would move a world no other cause,
Can be more plain for motion laws;
That planetary life assumes,
The sun and stars that space illumes
If sun is magetism to the earth,

In direct rays to give the birth,
Of germ life that the sun doth hold
And on earth's surface 'round enfold;
That troop from Nature's hiding places
Up into light and life's sweet graces;
Doth not the poles from north star draw
Electricity through similar law,
This electricity producing cold
That 'round the frigid zone enfold?
And turns the world around, around,
That electricity is natural bound
To curve in motion—while the sun
Throws rays in straight lines, every one?
Of different elements we see
Are sun rays from electricity;
Something associated with it
That will not its supremacy permit,
For one through glass will pass as well;
The other from it will repel;
And so the north star may be made
Of electricity's positive grade
Of elements that fill the pole,
A positive element and cold;
While the direct line of the sun,
Upon the torrid zone is one
Of many causes heat is found,
Upon the earth to there abound;
Uniting with the depths of air,
That growth attracts around it there;
The sun rays in the air we find,

And fills it with life-germs of mind,
Associated with electricity
From the sun, we cannot see;
That moves the sunlight in straight lines,—
The stronger principle of mind;
'Tis that associated with it,
Superior motion it will get;
'Tis mind the motion with it bound
When four things were in sun-ray found
By science analyzing it,
They found four elements in one
That in the sun-ray to us come;
The mind germs that to earth is given
From out the starry dome of heaven.
Two gases in the air explain
How they united make the rain;
Oxygen and hydrogen unite
And create water sparkling bright;
Could those gases ere contain
Germ life in the drop of rain?
That through a microscope is seen
Living life germs sport and gleam;
Out of water, sun and mud
"Upward troop the the lily's bud,
And in the higher brightness
Gathers all its lily's whiteness;"
So are germs sown from the air
In the earth that meeting there;
Find conditions for their being
To unfold in larger seeing;

Personal they start to grow
And a larger body know;
As it burst its atom cell,
Of its species it did tell,
As to larger life it grew;
This was life beginning new,
In primeval time we say,
And on islands new, to-day.
But as we absorb life, those
Germs that atom life compose,
Of our species we contain
And have conditions just the same,
That to-day our bodies hold
All life atoms so untold,
Thus developed is the stage
Of progressive life, this age;
Life germs have a higher way
For beginning life to-day;
Something higher than the earth,
For its mother-natal birth.
Parentage in nature strives
To protect advancing lives;
In her care she makes secure
Provisions that may life endure.

PROGRESSION OF LIFE ORIGIN.

FLESH is atoms used before,
    In life repetition o'er;
That thus develop more to bring
Out thought conditions in every thing;

Germs develop higher mind,
Because conditions they can find,
To unfold and yield to life,
And not confine its motions rife
With materials as coarse
As the earth, our primal source.
Thus to-day we have the man
That so much can understand;
Of the realms of space explore,
Where its life germ was before,
Ere it came into this being,
Personal for higher seeing;
Ere it mastered thought and mind,
Growing more in God to find.
Man in spaces comprehend
And through distance speech extend.
Until he is proving how
Ever present, thought is now
By electric made to be,
In an instant o'er the sea;
Or again to understand
Speech, and hear across the land;
Making omnipresent thought
Almost in itself outwrought;
Making machinery to do,
Work—without the feeling, too;
Such has mastered human mind,
More and better things to find;
As the ages still advance,
As we take a backward glance;

Growing more in God to find
All there is in that of mind;
When all this you can express,
This is growth in " godliness."
We have almost burst the shell
Of material where we dwell,
It has grown so thin to be,
With electric mind so free,
That we hear the speech of those
That to higher life arose;
Thought transference, which we find,
Is a higher sense of mind;
By this power we hear from those
That from matter have arose,
And find beyond our mortal ken
Life has being without end,
Nothing dies or does decay,
Atoms flee from each away,
Until the mortal body fade
Out of sight that has displayed,
Such solid substance, moved by mind
Which left it to another find,
More adapted to its might,
Growing up into the light;
From the darkness of the earth,
Revealing mind in greater worth;
Blossoms it may yet unfold
In the brighter light of gold,
Which it reaches up on high;
This is all it is to die,

H

Mind has entered higher brightness
To unfold unfettered lightness,
Where it is not held, but free
To reach its own inherency;
In the ages yet to come,
Beautifying every one;
With the powers of grander thought,
When the mind is more outwrought;
Just above this earth of ours
Mind has scope for higher powers,
There eventually to outgrow
Hereditary tendencies below,
Which we take from the material,
Impress left on the ethereal.

PROGRESSION OF ATOMS.

MATERIALS that have been used o'er and o'er,
Mind affinitized with before;
Materials that were thought impressed
Before in bodies, more or less;
Ere they were for us to bring
Out through it, our unfolding.
A means through which our life could be
Held,—and self assertion see;
And the impress on them wrought
Tends to lean that way our thought;
Thus our mind is warped to bring,
Out our inate unfolding;

While materials which we use
And from which we have to choose,
Have heredity of thought,
Long ago upon them wrought;
That have been the servants too
Minds of anger—made them do;
Or of drunkenness and sin,
That materials have within
The impressions on them made
By the life of every grade;
That the same materials wrought
In their bodies moved by thought;
The materials used by them,
Which we take and use again;
And were used the same before
Since the feeblest life had power
Over matter to unite
In a body for their might
Of ruling—to their will obey;
Materials have progressed this way,
By adaptation to the thought,
That has o'er and o'er them wrought;
'Till it reaches us to find
It is yielding more to mind.
It fetters not this mind of ours
As when mind had shown lesser powers;
Now adapts itself to motion,
That some represent the notion,
That we will not ever die,
Bodies too will upward fly;

So etheral they become,
That the two will meet as one;
Fitted for ethereal life.
But we feel the mind of strife,
Will surmount the one of clay
And go out and in as may
Be their will to go or come,
As two bodies held in one.
Each now sever ties that bind
And go out the human mind
To a broader field explore,
Of ethereal being more,
And return to this again,
And no death—this would explain.
'Tis our bodies laid aside
Now that death the two divide;
And to know these fields of air
And its limits everywhere;
Would our earth experience be
Ere we passed from this to stay;
In eternal being pure,
Life where ever will endure
What composes us of mind,
Those conditions yet to find;
Neither death nor yet decay
Would associate this way;
With clear seeing this will see—
Known while here what is to be;
And no death would thus divide,
Father, mother, sister, bride,

Husband, brother, friends of earth,
Have but risen to a birth;
Where the light of sun and air,
Higher brightness doth compare.

As the seed contains the tree,
What its growing yet will be,
When from out the seed to swell
And to higher brightness rise;
Where it sees the sun and skies,
Out of moisture earth that bore
Its existence there before.

THE USEFULNESS OF THE MATERIAL BODY.

So to us the earth has need,
As the darkness to the seed,
But when higher we arise
To the brightness of the skies,
Mind will need not then the clay
To withold its active ray,
In embodiment to rest,
'Till it can itself progress,
To advance its self-hood powers
Growing of this life of ours,
To the period of thought,
When self action it has wrought;
Why could not its self-hood grow,
In the spirit atom so?

When in action it was free
It moved right on most easily,
But when bound and could not stir
In material-inert power,
Then its self-hood had to grow,
The only motion it could know;
For 'twas natural to motion,
And vent itself in self promotion,
When its motion in material,
Was held—it self grew the ethereal;
And a body soon you see,
Of material personality,
With a force—life motion bound
In material clothed around,
The means that Nature took you know,
For our consciousness to grow.
The spirit atom she must bind,
That it might grow in self of mind,
To larger personality,
And all its mind inherency.
This law the horticulturists find
Will make a growth if they can bind,
Some part of plant life to defy,
And thus has grown the " Kohl Rabi."
Life its motion will assert
In some way if 'tis held inert.
When its self advancement wrought
Up to where it grew in thought,
Higher up it moved to when
Revealed to be,—women and men;

Highest type of mind to be
Gathering still its destiny;
Of the thinking powers of mind,
When the spirit-land doth find;
'Cumbered no more freely give
Action which is mind to live,
For electrical its motion
Would continue in promotion.

PRIMITIVE MOVEMENT OF LIFE.

LIFE self motion will assert
    But it must be held inert;
If in self-hood it would grow
In material atom so
It was bound a central force
That the atom held at first,
In lifes progress upward tending
The divine in us was sending;
That inherent central force,—
Atom mind of "Central Source,"
And when conditions had as right
The positive and negative atom unite;
The principals of female and male,
That in all Nature and space prevail;
And their union still would be
Natural to personality;
In life motion to unite,
Into one of motion quite

Electrical—of moving power.
Opposites will tend to give
Motion in all things that live;
So self motion it possessed,
When in union could not rest,
And advancing upward climbed
In the personal of mind,
With a dual nature growing
All self added powers bestowing.

SPACE AND AIR.

THE elements from space doth give
    The atoms through which all can live;
By their selections growth will there
Draw atoms from space to make the air,
What all material growths expel,
The air becomes, of that as well.
New atoms fill this waste of life,
Expelled in changes constant, rife
With growth—and so the unseen air
Has all within it everywhere
That growing life can thus unfold,
That any form within can hold;
Sustaining energies for growth,
As well as for material forms;
That clothes the spirit and adorns
The ever growing life within,
That always heretofore has been

An atom in the realms of space,
Until it found this growing place.
The waste thrown off by you,—will see
Accepted by some other life;
To form their bodies changing rife,
In varied substance to exchange
Relationship with all life range
That we in contact, live or touch,
Where both will be affected much,
If they in correspondence are,
With us either near or far.
Results for us, will either be
For good, if not a misery.
So each life seeks its own to find
The happiness of growing mind;
And if it finds its like will be
The chords of perfect harmony ;
Attuned by concert with our mate,
What we alone appreciate.

MATERIALISM.

OBJECTORS say conditions make
The mind—that principle alone;
Then how are different species known
When both have the same circumstances?
Alike they will not grow or be
But different species you will see.

If the material, made the mind
No different species you would find.
They like in body would unite,
When circumstance were alike;
In twins no difference would be,—
But most unlike—you often see.
Side by side two plants may grow,
And each selects its own to blow;
Its life identity is there
Within the seed—and colors rare;
Each life selecting from the same,
Shows different life the seed contained;
And their identity is shown,
When each bursts forth and larger grown;
And so it is with life that you
Hold in identity as true;
You both may use the self same air
And food, and bodies not compare.
If bodies made the human mind,
The same conditions you would find
Would make two species just alike;
But each selects from out the same,
What he appreciates,—contain
In each, a very different shape,
The self same elements would make.
So mind made you and was the force
The atom started with of course;
The mental atom making mind,
With all its added powers combined;
As it unfolded more and more,
From what it ever was before;

Concealed within an atom force
In energy—the living source
Of life, within the boundless whole;
We see in Infinite control
The system of the universe.

THE UNIVERSAL BODY.

IN all its planetary course,
    Of moving life and energy;
Atomic certain it must be;
And it harmonious is with law
That toward a center all things draw;
A living body it must be
Composed of atoms, same as we.
The elements are going 'round,
Bodies in space are moving found;
Attraction moves them 'round the one,
That strongest draws—planet or sun,
For all is life and motion given
There is no still in earth or heaven;
It all in motion has a course,
A universe of central force.
We see its system and we know
A universe of life doth go
Around a Central Moving Force,
And worlds and suns are in its course.
His living body—Nature's Mind,
Diffused throughout the whole we find;

" All parts of one Stupendous Whole,"
Filled with all germs that life unfold
To larger bodies,—we may grow,
But atoms still in God we know;
We are but parts His person fill,
As atoms are controlled by will;
Of universal system-laws,
Whose forces move, but have a cause,
If we compare His life to us,
The atoms of His body must
A system be moved by His will;
And everywhere His impulse thrill;
So we unite with His and we
Obey His will, what e'er it be.
Involuntary impulse all!
Which we appreciate—so small;
In waves of compensation laws,
Where all effects result from cause.
As the animalcule in us
In life courses may be thus,
Could not comprehend our mind,
But a force moving, might find;
As atoms in our body move,
Involuntarily with love;
And moving forces so express
A harmony with all the rest.
Touch but an atom 'tis the same,
It thrills at once unto the brain;
And motion sets up to relieve,
And carry off what doth aggrieve.

So we are parts of God entwined—
A universe of all combined;
And so related all are we,
That not a pulse can thrill, but He
Feels the impression great or small,
Joy, pain, or sadness, throughout all.
If all are parts of one grand whole
Connected all are with His soul;
And sending thought to Him from thee,
A wave comes back, as if to free
Thee in thy individuality;
And equalize what'er it be.

COMPENSATION.

IN compensation, ere it comes,
   With many unbelieving ones
They never realize that grief
Should come to them—and wish relief;
Although they have to others given
Sorrows that may have been heart-riven.
And time may pass before this comes,
Ere the wave doth reach the shore,
Reacting back where struck before;
Back on the source that suffering gave,
In compensation's moving wave.
And if 'twas joy, it gives the one
Who gave it more where it begun.

So compensation is the law,
That all have noted if they draw
Close conclusions and observe
That nothing can avert, or swerve
From this great tendency to draw
Through action and reaction law.
These moving purposes, in time,
Will teach a moral law to mind
That will inevitably entail,
And teach results that never fail.
And better be for what 'twill bring,
And help relieve all suffering;
For surely these effects return
To primal source that lessons learn.
As light reflects and shoots across—
A shadow on 'till it is lost,
Reflects and back to sources come,
Where action starts, from every one;
And energy, a ceaseless force,
Moves onward, all within its course;
So we are moving by Divine
Omnipotence, the central mind.

CIRCLING MOTION.

AND distance has no end, but round
And full of bodies, all is found
To move in circles, so the years
Revolve throughout eternal spheres.

Time is but something we call time
That spaces mark between the worlds,
But in supposing there were none
To mark a distance there is some,
Something that fills distance whirled;
Life motion also stirs the worlds
That live in space, as dots that flow
Around, because all distance go
In this life motion, as the source
Of undivided central force.
And all within it follow laws,
In symbol of this " Primal Cause."
Our bodies are a dual one,
The male and female both become
A unit life, so God must be
In principals the same as we;
Atomic bodies us compose,
But single mind o'er it arose.

UNDIVIDED MIND AS A UNIT.

TO be the unit moving force,
    So life has bodies like its source,
Cut off the arm,—'tis atom made,
'Twill not this principal invade;
We feel our body as a whole,—
A unit power, you call it soul;
We care not what the name may be,
A unit mind enclosed have we;

And this identity of mind
Is what we keep through endless time.

SENSATION OF ATOMS.

WE know the body has a range
  Of constant and material change;
Atomic formed—some doth compose
Those of feelings—some are those
That are not the nerves to mind—
Bone and sinew some combine;
But they ever go and come
New, for old, supplies each one;
In the constant ever change,
That ethereal minds arrange,
To upbuild the body where
Its selection places there;
Some more active to his mind,
Carrying thoughts as they combine,
To the extreme of finger tips,
Or voiced in moving of the lips,
Which of atoms are as those
Which some other part compose,
In the brain or nervous cells,
Action and reaction—expells
Atoms which these thoughts compose,
To supply their place with those
That are new—but in this wise,
Atoms see if they are eyes,

Atoms feel if they are nerve,
While unto the mind they serve;
As they go and as they come,
Have experiences, each one,
That are those of atom life,
Surging with the forces rife;
When with mind in love they come
Responsive—atoms do become;
To express the mind of thought
That these atoms drew and wrought,
In material bodies where
They as servants to him there
Must have listened, to obey,
And progressed in this same way,
To sensations of a thought,
Which attracted them and wrought
Out a body, like the one
They are yielding, too, become
By the will and force of mind,
They in yielding, too, combine;
Making different forms of yore,
Those they helped to make before;
Different bodies thus express
The ethereal one they dress.
Then where we have been before
Making bodies o'er and o'er,
And exchanging love with mind
Atoms feel when they combine,
With the thoughts of lives before,
That have used materials o'er,

I

Reincarnated with each life;
Sense their joy, or feel their strife,
Active with a mind we know
Of its wants and of its woe;
For its feelings we express,
Some the more and others less,
Words the mind willed us to do;
This has been the life of you,
Ere you came into this one,
Where your consciousness begun;
Where your selfhood larger grew,
And added life power came to you,
Movement—whose results were breathing,
New conceptive life perceiving;
Was awakened from this motion
Of the life power through promotion;
Which resulted in the mind,
New effulgences to shine.
Breathing that outside of you
Gave your being something new,
A connective power with space—
Sunlight, air and all you trace
Of its elements unfold,
To you come, and you behold
All there is outside of thee.
'Tis called consciousness by thee;
In the breathing—thought combined
In the chemistry, with mind.

THE PHILOSOPHY OF SLEEP.

WHAT is sleep? I hear you say,
　　Sleep induces in this way;
If the mind would close its door,
You asleep were, as before,
When you were in fetal life;
Infant life power it retains,
All mind ever had remains;
Power that mind has in its ways
To return to youthful days,
Mind unable to project,
Backward it can still reflect;
It retains primeval power,
Sleep projects to thoughtful hour;
So the mind holds its control,
In protection of the soul;
All it held—the thinking powers,
With its sleep and waking hours;
In vibrating action giving,
To inertia then to living,
To material—then to mind,
Each upon the other climbed;
One power on the other bring,
As winter lapses into spring.
One in love of sleep was resting,
The other from it—was divesting,
In the active power of thought;
Until from each the other drew,
And each their own love to pursue.

Life to seek the realms of mind,
And untrammeled action find;
While all the atoms of material,
In separation, became ethereal
As the air and did not stay
In a body, but fled away;
When the stage that you call death—
Life, out of material left;
The atoms each from each expelled,
For nothing drew them, nothing held,
When the life had left them there
Soon they were again the air.
This is how our life advances,
When its self growth takes its chances;
When in atom life it stays,
Then more quiet are its ways,
'Till moved by higher forces—when
It obeys those forces then,
Of whatever life may draw
Them through love it never saw;
Ere it grew itself to be
A larger personality;
Ere its life had thus progressed,
And millions other lives had dressed,
With a physical, and they
Had learned the mind power to obey.

ROMANCE OF AN ATOM.

IN all bodies we have lived;
  To the trees and flowers have given
The rose hues that have expressed,
The life-rose that it has dressed;
So life atoms have before
Been in bodies o'er and o'er;
And together well have made
Statures tall that thought displayed;
As it served the will of mind,
Did its biddings thought enshrined;
'Till perceptible it were,
To whatever did occur,
As it acted with the mind,
Thrilled with pleasure—or defined
Problems grand, through human speech,
As to thought realm it did reach;
And produce the thought again,
That was formed within the brain,
Where the seat of mind held sway,
And dictated day by day;
Going out or coming back
As mind servants they did act,
All along the concert line,
Each vibrating thought of mind,
To its neighbor next to it,
'Till the surface they did get.
Uttering in a speech, the word
That in speech of mind had heard.

This, material atoms have done
In the body of each one,
It has ever lived in where,
It vibrated thought and prayer;
For if paralyzed was one,
Servants for his thoughts have none,
In those parts where speech is done;
Thus in the body, atoms find
Work to do for human mind;
Acting for its unseen friend—
Diplomat it did attend;
At the doorway, through the hall,
Carrying news to give to all;
Uttering speech in lips that said,
Eyes that looked the thought instead;
We the servants have been made,
In the life of every grade;
'Till we reach the season when—
We were servants unto men.
So impressed has been our life,
When in atoms we were rife,
We have lived those same scenes o'er,—
Where our life has been before;
Ere we made your body where
Your sweet mind so soft and fair,
Touched us with its sympathy,
And you reflected back from me
Something like heredity;
'Tis materials that enshrine
Acts sometimes upon the mind;—

Sentiments on them impressed
Some the more and others less;
For you never lived before
But in atoms, o'er and o'er
You have lived in groups with those,
Acting what another knows;
This was first your human mind,
With humanity in form,
Where you larger grew to be,
All that mind in you can see,—
Breathing, thinking, conscious life,
Seeing, hearing, all the strife,
And have grown to be the king,
Over atoms which you bring,
For your body, to compose.
Which will act for you—as those
That once governed you in life,
When you were an atom rife
In a body doing will;
You are living, acting still;
But outside your body see;—
By breathing—this has come to thee,
A connected power attain,
With sunlight, air, and all you gain,
By unfolding higher powers
In breathing motion, which is ours
With the chemistry of mind;
All our consciousness we find;
Elements that life unfold,
To you come and you behold

In expression of the mind,
This new thought world, which you find;
To develop reason, sense,
Where you came from, whither, whence,
You are journeying, all's a stage,
Of some state and life and age.
No life ever did begin,
We are atoms all of Him;—
God who is the whole we see
Universe, and all is He,
And His body has control
Has its seat and central soul.
We the servants of his mind
Always will with Him combine.
Ever will be as we soar,
Circling on forevermore;
On in knowledge we will be,
Parts of its immensity,
We His system all will fill,
And be atoms in Him still;
When we reach the highest stage
We can think of future age.
It is true the Prophet said
" In His image we were made,"
Atoms in us every grade;
Animalcule life through all,
Makes our bodies great and small.
Will is force of the mind;
Force as in space combined;
Moving energy and strife,
'Round the Central Force Of Life.

Brain is central of the mind;
And connected motion find,
With all parts, its courses run,
In the personal become.
So the Universal Mind,
Central moves the whole combined,—
Universal system, where
All is life in space and air;
And a correspondence find
In God and forces of the mind;
For all the universe is moving
'Round some center-worlds are proving;
Force invisible is power;
Mind explains this every hour;
As our thoughts the mind illume,
So the flower yields its perfume;
Both invisible exhale
Life force, of a different scale;
Central mind gives off this power,
Acting, as perfume the flower.
Magnetism is a thing
Unseen—yet its forces bring
Strength and substance, so to hold
Cords of unseen substance fold
'Round us, so we know and feel
Substance, which does not reveal
To the sight, but still we know
They with unseen atoms flow;
Unseen substance sure must be,
Alike those that we can see;—

Are atomic in construction
That conceal in their production,
Spirit atoms—infant minds
Which in unseen forces binds.
Drawn by affinity and will,
In concert acting—forces still.
So the universe is moved
By unseen forces it is proved;
For electricity is one
Of the forces which become;
To our senses something there,
Filling all through space and air;
It must be atomic in construction;
And spirit atoms are from its production.
So all substance of thought grade
Is of spirit atoms made,
And all substances unseen
Flowing in magnetic stream
Through the body, moved by mind.
So in space and stars we find
Moving in the space between
Planets, there is that unseen
Magnet, that to us appears
Nothing—through the orbit spheres;
All is substance of thought grade,
And of spirit atoms made;
Making substances unseen,
Moving in the space between
Planets orbits through the spheres;
All is substance which appears

To be nothing, when unseen;
But expression in the gleam
Of electric light, that there
Is expression in the air
Of a substance, like a thought
That will presence show when brought
Into usefulness, or bound
Move on lines, or whirling 'round.
Particles will so unite
That love and hate express to sight,
From unseen forces which unite
Them into a substance seen,
In affinity to move;
It expresses in it love,
Or hate which sensations use,—
As its course of will pursues;
Both these natures, higher thought
Use still more in bodies wrought.
This would show that atom minds
In attractive forces binds;
Mind concerts its unseen will,
On the atoms which doth fill
The nervous fluid in its course—
The electric substance—Force.
And they follow in its course;
In their sense of love and hate
Meeting mind, they thus relate,
Now my romance to pursue
Of the atom life and view,
And its story longer tell
Where it soared and where it fell.

We present the mind to view
When we shape the face of you,
Its revelations make and thus
Frowns and smiles are made by us;
Lisped in wail or dying moan,
On face where wretchedness is shown,
That may well a thought compose,
Expression on the face it throws,
That drew the picture of the mind
Upon the features, shade and line,
As servants of his will obey;
On the material to display
What the atoms understood;
To shape in concert, then they would;
When adapted to the thought
Of mind that had the body wrought.
Once an atom I was where
Disease, had pierced the body there;
Or happened there at that same time
Within the elements enshrined;
Mind great efforts made to throw
Off waste substance that was so
Inactive, in the vital part,
It could no longer stir the heart.
Then life took its outward flight
And death had stilled the form—to sight;
Her, my complement and bride
Two, we were, worked side by side;
Paired were we—revolving 'round
In life currents—loving bound;

What consternation when we saw
That life had answered to a law,
That we were left without a will,
Or governing power, for all was still.
The mind had left its body then;
To get out of the shape of men
Was next our feelings—so to do;
But life did not expel us through
Its courses—as it had before,
And we must stay till all was o'er;
'Till atoms thought to take their part
And strive from each one—each to start;
And as we did this pleasure seek
Of our own feelings not a week,
Were we confined to stay so still,
We each expressed our own sweet will;
And soon we were again in air,
And earth, and winds, and everywhere;
And heard the call of bees and flowers,
And languished through the summer hours;
And fanned a gentle maiden's cheek
That loved our whisperings to seek,
She drew us in her sighing breath,
Where loves sweet voice, could find no death;
We sported on through nerves to find
The feelings of another mind;
And in a loving tender thought,
We seemed of this same substance wrought,
And given out in loving word,
Receptive there another heard,

And drew us in his fondest thrill
Of sentiments, that seemed to fill
His being, then with active power
It seemed with mind to be then, our
Mission, 'till we knew, or seemed
To know, our substance was unseen,
For we were substance of a thought,
And feeling, which was then enwrought;
And seemed prophetically to see
A day ahead when we might be,
Grown ourselves to be a mind
Receptive to a thought, inclined
In consciousness, that we might be
A larger individuality;
And in a living thought to thrill,
And find conditions where we will
From out our atom cell—be grown;
And more of real existence known;
When we could leap as do the flowers,
Up from the seed to higher powers;
Through the change, unconscious be;
Outshone by higher individuality.
In life's bright scenes so new, forget
Awhile, where atom life had slept;
Emblazoned by this life so new,
That breathing motion to us drew
From space and sunlight—newly born
Into a realm, so much adorn
Outside of self hood, where we drew,
Our first existence, to the new

Conditions, where our life would grow,
Out of the atom—more to know;
As we increased to higher power
And motion added, as the flower
From out an atom seed, will grow
To be a stalk and leaf and blow,
Upon its topmost highest stem,
Yielding perfume, as thoughts in men,
Is product of their highest life;
When it inhales from air and sun,
And form has grown, from that begun;
Primevally an atom small
That never did begin at all,
For it was ever an atom mind
In Universal Forces, where
It was in God an atom there
And ever His great form we fill
And are to him as atoms still;
But living in a different state
Of life, more observations make;
And ever will as on we soar
In God and conscious evermore;
As elements our life inhale,
A motion that in life prevail;
Will still continue as we reach,
In elements, no words of speech
Can be expressed on earth, to you
Where limited is yet your view,
Of what the universe contains
Of beauty in its broader range.

THE UNIVERSE.

The universe has central force,
And central mind—of all mind source;
And omnipresent outward flows,
Through all and every thing it goes;
Alike have atoms central power,
And are a unit of mind dower;
If units form all substance seen
Would not the unseen be the same?
Electricity we can name,
As one that you must comprehend
As atomic, where more extend,
Higher, finer, those there be,
That are still yet unknown to thee;
This is the basic of our plan,
Where individual starts in man;
As well as everything you see
That has life personality.
In man's invincible of mind,
That in material forms we find
A unit force, that to them draw
Materials, by attraction law.
Attraction is a force of love
In atoms as in forms above,
And by their hate expel away
Those, after using—every day;
Thus all the while he gains a new
Material body, through and through;

But always the same mind, retains
In person.—This you see explains
Why the material changing new,
Shapes always, the personal of you.
For if a person was not there
Within, to place them everywhere
That in selections it has made,
For every part, its proper grade;
How could they come together so,
That your same personal could know;
What force but mind could be selecting
From everywhere, and be protecting
Your same looks, and person too?
When this thought carefully you view.
Mind must discriminate and draw,
These atoms by its love—the law,
To clothe itself—They form its shape;
And when mind leaves it, they escape
And do not then in forms unite,—
The atoms of material, right
For bodies, that will mind express,
In life and thought-moving, unless
A central force, as power of mind
The atoms do again combine;
And then it is another shape
Of looks and face to imitate;
The same species may disclose
Something similar to those;
And be a unit life of mind
Within materials combined,

But a life atom different still
In thought and looks its presence fill,
An atom force with body small,
And growing larger this is all;
There is to make a person there
Out of materials coarse and rare;
That doth compose the flesh and bone,
Or nerves, that have more feeling shown,
With mind, so atoms differ much
With thought sensation, by the touch
Of mind upon them, quick respond,
Intelligent, connective bond;
While others cannot feel or show,
The least sensation that you know,
Conveyed to you, from outer strife,
To citadel, of conscious life;
The central seat of mind in power,
Dominant person, over our
Whole system, but the seat of mind,
In one location, central find,
Within the orbit of the head,
Almost a round—but where 'tis fed
With body, sending out a part
Of circulation with the heart;
As a machiney reaches long,
To gather in and move more strong;
So mind connects with body through,
That will more surface ground explore;
And gather in, increasing more
Than what it could if it were round,
And in circumference small were bound.

Thus bodies feed the mind and hold
Their sentinels, which they unfold,
When they have burst the cell of mind,
A body does project to find
The higher gains of life to be;
As from the round seed bursts a tree,
It is a higher form of life;
As larger surface it reveals;
For surface of the body feels,
So feeling is sensation more
Than what your life was in before,
It did a larger form express,
And in material you were dressed.
It is protected and obscure
In darkness, 'till it can endure,
By being conscious unto pain;
Itself in matter must remain.
Matter is non-conductor to
Forces invisible to you.
Conditions life-growth doth prepare,
That life its conscious self, declare;
So in the darkness of material,
Expanded the life-growth of ethereal;
With the material so combined,
That there can be self-growth of mind.
Nature all her forms conceal
In darkness, to the first reveal;
Life in starting growth to be
Protected, and in blindness be;
To have conditions first to grow
On what we call the earth below;

And blinded to the light supreme,
That brighter life above us gleam;
Where we will rise as from the earth
And darkness—up a seed is burst
" As from the rocks and earth and mud
Upward troop the lily's bud,"
And gather in this higher brightness,
All the lily's purest whiteness,
So we will rise from earth and clay
Into the light of purer day;
And gather beauty of the soul,
That will the brightest mind unfold,
In beauty of inherent power,
As on the treetop blooms the flower;
And then the loveliness will see,
Of what our life was made to be;
And God the Author and the Source
Of life in us—we'll love of course;
And feel a constant joy to know
More of ourselves than here below;
To comprehend these higher powers
Of life—seen more and more in ours.
All of ourself will be divine,
To be an atom of His mind,
And we would God love as ourself,
When we a part of him would be,
In correspondence you must see,
To be an atom of His mind,
The spark of life must be divine;
To be a unit of His mind,

That fills the universe with love;
Such is the God we know above;
To live and to immortal be,
Will be rejoicings you will see
That fills the bosom of your life.

THE HIGHER LIFE.

ABOVE—when meet husband and wife,
    Mothers and fathers, brothers, where
Sisters and friends will all be there;
Rejoicings, for they feel and know,
A clearer vision than here below.
They now observe, can see the end
That greater love and joys extend,
On to the Infinite extreme,
Where greater bliss in living seems.
Where fairest flowers and song of birds
And loving harmonies of words,
And softest winds, whose lulling sound
Vibrates with music all around;
Where bowers of roses—sweet perfume
Select from all the choicest bloom;
Wafts to your sense and seem to lull
You in conditions with the whole,
And fills your being with delight,
As though a glow of purest light
Enveloped you with purest joy,
Without the sorrow of alloy,

Or even thought of shade could bring
The smallest cloud of silvered ring;
Such is our bliss in highest life,
That we have reached beyond all strife.
Where unknown things would us obscure,
Now reason lights with knowledge pure;
And love so perfect all doth fill,
We meet with its magnetic thrill,
Unknown to any joy below,
It fills the air harmonious so
To our being's electric thrill;
Its ecstacies cannot be shown
By any thing that you have known.
Such are the highest joys of living,
That highest worlds of life are giving;
All its attaining joys doth teach
The lowest life to higher reach;
For life is struggling e'er to find
The greatest happiness of mind,
And this doth reach in worlds above,
And draws them upward through its love.
Where life culminates complete,
Heaven and earth doth truest meet.
But where are those that have not made
The perfect plane of higher grade,
That started out perhaps with you?
Some now are learning lessons new,
To their advantage, how to reach
The heights experiences teach;
Who chose their way through different sight
Of ways, to reach this higher light.

All gain these heights to the Supreme
In channels of a different stream,
That ever outward, onward flows
With different means and ways for those
That saw not God or felt His thought,
Through Nature in His being wrought,
As parts of you can feel your mind,
And thrill responsive with it act,
Take different routes, but reach with those
Parts where the circulation goes,
When they have gained the highest part
Of mind and pulsing with the heart;
Will feel its all prevading love;
So we feel God in heights above;
So we will reach the worlds sublime,
And glow of Infinite thought mind,
And thrill with its magnetic love,
Responsive in bright worlds above.
And every thing in God will reach
These worlds that experiences teach;
And all must feel it great or small
In conscious life attained by all.
Progression is God's circulation,
All reach yet the same destination.
Different each are different made,
And all life is a different grade
Of life identity, but all gain
The perfect growth and it retain,
Like fruit upon the orange tree,
Some ripe, while others green may be,
The ripe ones only you call good.

DEVELOPMENT.

BUT all will yet be understood
   To be the same, but want the time
To reach its ripening, fair and fine;
And so all things are yet the good,
When life-work well is understood.
The smallest life that you may know
Is yet immortal on to grow,
Each flower and vegetable and tree,
And animals, as well as thee;
And worlds and all that they become
In rock and crystal that have begun.
All motion that asserts a life,
And moving in severest strife,
Will yet develop parts that lay
In dormancy, some future day;
By simply living, yet will grow
Out of conditions, where you know
Their life to be as you behold;
And shine as pure as perfect gold.
From all alloy they yet will reach
That have obscured some parts of each;
And freedom will to life express
Inherent traits, showing less
Unbalanced actions—full in mind;
Will show themselves—will yet abound
With those that long ago have found;

And when they do, that life will show
A harmony of lovely glow,
As to the bass notes you would give,
Soprano power in what doth live;
The whole keyboard of sound—in full
Out of the worst sound there could be;
Would concert sound make harmony,
And so with life, the worst that may
Be seen will grow some future day,
In all life organs of mind force,
Result in beauty yet—of course.
So God an evil never made,
But laws of growth in every grade
Of life express different parts,
What conditions gave the start;
And action was the law of force,
And life expressed the combination
In all variety of creation;
What'er it was in concert there
Of organs, gave life everywhere,
Of different shapes, to its desires,
That kept life concert—inward fires,
And if 'twas greed, to build it would
Its shape to gain the most it could;
For bodies show the inward soul,
And mind and thought that has control;
And physiognomy reads it right,
When it compares the features where
The coarse, or fine, expresses there;
And if 'twas fear that had its growth,

Life force within its body shaped,
Unto its needs to best escape,
The ears constructed well to hear
The slightest sound approaching near;
And built the limbs for action fleet,
The slim and strong and tiny feet.
As in the deer we see the build
Betokening what the mind instilled,
The parts where growth of mind has been
And in heredity extend;
To shape the physical and aid
This power in mind the form has made
For it, controls the atoms there
Supplying waste in its repair;
And thus the body from the start
Expresses freedom, for this part
Of motion, given by the mind,
And physiognomy reads its kind.
The lion with destructive power
Has built its jaws to best devour,
So mind expresses where 'tis grown,
What organs full can well be known,
And what are dormant, yet to grow,
Can well be read when this you know;
The base with the soprano tone
Must join where melody is known.
The symmetry of human mind,
Compared to animals we find,
That first existed on the earth,
With life in its primeval birth.

SELFISHNESS.

WHY does the selfish part of mind,
    Develop first ? The cause we find,
Productive to survival life,
To overcome its crowding strife,
Must start the selfish plane of thought,
Where life continuance is sought;
The base of growth before the one
That higher growing will become.
For selfishness tends to survive
Through persistant growth, all the alive;
Would they continue, they must feed
Themselves, so this trait all must need;
As they ascend, the base is filled,
With higher traits that on them build;
So selfishness the lowest grade
Of mind, first manifestation made;
And it essential is to life,
In all the struggles of its strife;
To reach the highest of desires,
That inward prompt ambition fires
Of character, this trait of mind,
In all, essential we will find
In union with the higher powers
Of character, as reason towers.

WHY THE FEMALE IS PHYSICALLY WEAKER.

TO heights of love,—Love drags them down,
    Where greatest selfishness surround;
'Tis seen in female for her young;
The farthest down where life begun,
Her love with that of self arose
In growth of mind,—We see in those
Of female sex, this weaker strength.
Divided 'twixt herself—at length
In offspring—made her to succumb
To selfish male, the stronger one.
Why? because the selfish he did feed
While she divided with her seed;
A higher trait of mind was brought
Down to the level of his thought;
That only he devoured to bring,
The elements all unto him;
And this is why the female race
In lowest life had weakest place;
She must have love to feed her young
And share with it 'till they become
Strong enough to her devour
In muscle of a stronger power;
If she had only stopped to feed;
Herself, then life could not succeed;
For she her offspring would devour,
As sometimes seen the present hour,
The male will feed himself on those,
Of offspring, where the selfish grows,

The strongest trait of his in mind,—
As animals some sorts and kind
To-day we see—In time to grow,
And leave the selfish plane below,
Whereon the higher traits can build
Of character by growth instilled.
To-day the race is weak because,
That higher man has from this cause,
Protected her weakness, from his love,
Until she has not raised above
Primeval stage in this, to show,
Development to higher grow;
And in heredity to-day
Has cultivated in this way;
As if 'twas life's best part to be
So delicate, instead of free
To grow in perfect life's full powers;—
Supporting stronger minds than ours;
Then would the race like ripened grain
Standing upright, in sun and rain,
Bear perfect grain to grow and be
Rich harvests of humanity.
By the unfoldment of this part
Of mind upon the first to start
Makes her now superior, in love nature
Her mind first gaining, this love feature;
When in concert action all,
When every trait of mind once small,
Will be full grown, then active strength,
Will raise above this vale at length;

And love and peace we grow into,
Is nearer God—whose love is through
The whole, in perfect unison;
Because in perfection, He is One;—
As harmony in all the spheres,
Wherein unchanging law appears;
That though we struggle in the strife,
And growing age of active life,
Meets it in waves of thought unknown
To its disturbance so outgrown;
Is God in its life Central Force.

HARMONY.

THROUGHOUT the whole the moving source;
That though a planet should explode,
The laws of space would move the same,
And not a ripple you could name,
Would mar its smooth and even sea
That comprehends eternity;
Only in compensation waves
The elements all discord saves;
Where great disturbance doth arise
The elements to equalize,
Throws back a sameness on the one
Whose action was the cause begun;
As action and reaction vies
The elements to equalize.
But these experience lessons teach,
That all intelligence can reach,

And feel whatever right to do
Where it again comes back to you;
" Do unto others as you would
That they do unto you " is good.
This compensation touches all
Where actions and reactions fall.
Such laws of harmony throughout,
Cannot injustice bring about;
If harmonious we would move,
In all the elements of love,
And peace that fills the whole sublime
Beyond the strife of smaller mind,
Love and justice must combine.

INVISIBLE DISTANCE.

THIS distance that with life is full
    Would still exist the same if all,
Were not within it great and small;
As much as arteries would flow,
The blood to veins and backward go,
In circulation moving on,
If every atom out were gone;
That in the blood-like atom worlds,
Around and 'round each other whirls.
So all in space disturbs not Him,
Whose presence fills unending space
With life and motion every place;
A system of perpetual power,
And life unto the present hour;

That we behold before us all
The presence of both great and small;
The universe of moving worlds,
That 'round and 'round each other whirls;
Thus all existing, what is the cause?
But life and its unending laws;
Embraced in system—moving true,
Invariable—all motion through
In which we live, and do partake
Of all its nature—systems make;
As atoms of " That Whole " we view—
This system was, long before you.
Of which your system grew to be
A symbol of the whole in thee,
Though we could never God become,
Nor could we ever grow to one,
For parts, could never whole embrace,
We would be atoms still in space,
Compared to what the whole must be,
Embraced in all Eternity,
Whose central force moves all around,
His larger system—so profound.
We symbolize from atom source,
The universe of central force.
All atoms have a central power,
As seeds resemble tree and flower,
In which their life has formed a part,
As offspring like its pulsing heart;
So we resemble the " All Source,"—
Our atom life has central force.

DUALITY OF ONE.

AND if two things in one unite;
    As two eyes blend into one sight;
Or two lobes of the brain produce
One blending of a mind in use;
So God this universe unfolds,
Two forces which its system holds,
To equalize as one we see,—
That active and reactive be.
Male and female we call its power
In motion as it rises higher,
These forces then we have in our
Motion, of one mind to grow,
And we resemble Him then so;
One universe, one mind remain,
Of dual elements the same,
The dual one, may both express—
The two that forms them more or less.
The universe one mind of motion
Express two forces in equal proportion,
All Father and all Mother love
That fills all Presence, here and above.
The positive and the negative course,
Must be the male and female force
Of Life, expressed in us unbalanced power,
Of elements that contra move
In atoms showing hate and love;

K

These all are tending more and more,
To equalize and one restore;
From two in parts to equalize,
One mind power that exactly vies,
In perfect balance of the one
When all into perfection come;
And ruled by love the perfect law
When all move where attractions draw;
As all the planetary force
Moves 'round one distant central source,—
Perfection in the universe.
For love doth like attraction draw
And this overcomes all other law;
And move in harmony to one,
Where love's attraction does become
The power that moves all things we see
Around one force—Immensity.
And so our minds may yet progress
To that perfection more or less,
That harmony of thought and love
May be the height attained above;
Where dominant hate enters not in
To be the product of a sin,
When we all error can release,
Will not the mind reach that of peace,
When we all undeveloped—leave,
Then harmony you will perceive.
For hate was once predominant thus
As selfishness was first in us,
Hate predominating destroys,
And love with balanced power is joy;

In dual one both as one vies,
In happiness to equalize.
When perfect love in growth attains;
As worlds of harmony explains,
Then sweet " Nirvana " is its joy,
Unchangable without alloy;
A joy that thrills the soul in bliss,
Of ecstacies unknown in this;
Where we beginning strive to know
What we can reach as on we grow.
But no beginning, we can see
If circles are Eternity;—
As higher risen into one—
Attract into the next begun;—
The Universal Whole, combined,
Impregnated with a force of mind.
Or magnetism we would call,
That's made of atom minds through all,
And forms a substance so refined
That 'tis unseen we call it mind.
But Undivided Whole must be
Of mind—All Presence Personality;—
A dominant mind the same as we.
Our magnetism is atom minds
Resembling us—and it combines
In force unseen, that we expel;
But still an undivided mind have we,
Embraced in our personality;
And by analogy we say
The universe is this same way.

An Omnipresent Mind is one
Thought, through all we see begun;
Every plan doth harmonize
In construction earth and skies;
As if one harmonizing thought
Throughout the whole each thing has wrought.
The form of man arteries and veins
Shaped like a tree—this thought explains
That does alike each thing express,
The same in all things more or less;
Great trunks and branches have each one,
Each will in contents, each become,
Through their relationship, will twine,
In tracery of sprays so fine,
And what the arterial tree contains,
Soon flows within the tree of veins;
As fine as moisture of each atmosphere,
Absorb one, from the other, here,—
One little universe of soul,
With many systems in its whole;
All moving in one power of mind,
As worlds and systems one combined;
As if one Universal Whole,
Alike expressed all things One Soul,
In its foundation principles;
Again, bodies round you see expressed
In all construction more or less;
The planets round and things we see
Are atoms round composing thee;
In all combined that man compose;
The head and eyes are round with those

Of atoms that combine to make,
The muscles if a chart you take
Of the anatomy, and compare
You find a sameness in us there
Of shapes of leaves, clusters of fruit,
Astonishing in its pursuit,
How much each part of us compose,
The shape of fruit and flowers, as those
That on the world's round body live;
Enrooted life, from germs that give
Themselves at first from air around,
The germs that in all space abound;
And mostly seed is round in form,
Before it bursts and life is born
Out of it, to more high express,
A form to feed its loveliness.
A force in space all present reigns
Invisible like mind remains,
Attracts around all things we see
It expressed, as drops will be
Shaped at once, round like a world
Or bubbles sport, or liquid hurled
From tower height melted lead will fall
Through space, and each drop form a ball;
It shows One ever present mind,
Expresses every thing combined,
Near a world, at least we see;
Unless world's magnetism it should be,
It may be, for far out in space
The feathery snowflake-stars embrace;

Yet flowers of snow they may be true,
As star-shaped flowers we often view.
A force invisible doth draw
In space, an action called a law
Harmonious motion everywhere,
One mind in nature would compare,
As undivided whole must be
This mind of Omnipotency,
And that its fullness moves the whole,
As mind in us expresses soul.
From this we claim that God must be
All present Personality,
For things this nature to express,
And we the parts of all the rest,
That does His energy compose
The forces that throughout all flows,
As in us magnetism combines,
Composed of substance—atom minds;
We have beside in us you see
This mind of our identity;
That every part of us embrace;
You cannot touch the smallest place
Upon our surface, but it will be
Made known to our personality;
And its infringement we expel,
If we are normal we can tell;
And always feel a perfect form
That to this feeling will conform;
This is our personality;
Unchangeable identity.

Besides the forces of life motion,
The product of the will and strength
Expressed in will may reach in space
In distance from us to entwine
Hypnotic states—the fruits of mind;   .
This proves a substance—so you see
Composed of atoms it would be,
Of atom minds—in nature-force,
A substance unseen like its source,
Of which our offspring may be known
Their minds resembling much our own,
And be the foundation of a life
That through unfolding enters strife,
When they in person grow to be,
From atom personality;
It seems a proof that we enfold
Magnetic substance atomic,
Because this substance, like the rest
Of substance, is a thing expressed;
Must be like others if we find
The substance gold—or like the mind;
Then if gold may atomic be,
Why not this magnetism, which we see,
Be atom minds, that this express,
A substance it is like the rest,
Only invisible like mind,
Its nature is of finer kind,
The invisible, the unseen.

ANALOGY OF SUBSTANCES.

THERE are other substances I could name,
    That are invisible the same,
Electricity a substance call,
If generated in a ball;
Invisible it too might be
Conducted where you do not see;
And yet as substance it would fill
Enough, sufficiently to kill;
And you could sense that this could be
A substance finer than you could see;
Might be atomic, like the rest
Of substances have been expressed.
Each atom of this electricity
Would be an unseen personality;
And what inherent it contained,
In growth of self would be explained;
And in a body act as force;
Like nature of the mind, of course.
A material substance you will take,
And call it atomic because it will break
In parts, invisible substances such we find,
(Except the personal of mind,)
The substance that a magnet fill
Will separate, and it will still
Be in the knife-blade to attract,
And in the magnet both will act;
The same in substance, the same kind,
And separate, where it combined

Within the magnet—to the blade;
And both have the same power displayed;
Attract the needle, so you see
If you can reason things must be
Atomic, because apart they break,
Then this invisible must make
Itself atomic, just the same;
As material substances explain.
It is much finer than material
This attraction force ethereal;
Through material it will go
The needle floating this will show,
This force will draw through it the same.
Attraction—spirit force is plain;
Passes through substances material,
Just like substances ethereal;
Atomic this substance must be composed,
In the magnet—as thought that flows
Into the material of another
And hypnotize them with its force,—
A substance—both must be, of course,
As much as gold or any gem
That is called atomic by all men.
It binds as strong as cords can bind,
This substance given by the mind;
Then why should thought not be expressed
As something atomic, unless
It should prove that we could be
Eternal in individuality—
Eternal because we ever were

An individual mind before,
In forces that doth never change
In all the universal range.
So personal would ever be
When added life power came to thee,
Expanding in identity,
And growing larger than before
Into all life proportions more,
And added power 'till we could be
Conscious, and surroundings see;
Because life motion in all breathing,
Drew in the elements perceiving;
When it in contact with the mind
Came as two forces, to combine;
The product of this combination,
Resulted in the thought creation;
And mind acceptance did create
The motion that it was awake;
And when rejecting, mind would sleep,
And mind its self-protection keep,
The same as it had been before,
Ere breathing action added more—
An ever growing power to mind,
As through material it did shine
Through the five senses leading to
This mind, secreted from all view,
Because "Dame Nature" does express
The life force in concealment dressed,
In self-security to rise
Upward slowly in disguise,

Until it could by feelings know,
Through pain and pleasure, how to grow.
The life of seeds she binds in shells,
And then the fruit around them swells,
So in the richness of decay,
A self-support from it—they may
Find—to make their body grow,
Concealed within its life—we know.
So Nature cares for all her own;
By " Mother Nature " she is known,
And us she folded in her care
Before we grew to what we are,
And ever still she watches yet,
And gives us that which life protects;
If we instinctive thought extend
To her, us great assistance lend,
To free us from disease and pain,
If we instinctive power retain,
And listen to the forces round
Us, so vision can be found
To guide our life in truthful ways,
And lengthen out our earthly days.
Just think one moment, if our air
Should different elements compare,
A little more from what they are,
United now, we might be far
From health, or even might not live,
Such perfect system she doth give
Of life to us,—Then think if we
Will not be hers eternally;

Our mother to us in all time,
With love as I confer on mine,
That are my children—only three,
While hers doth fill Immensity;
And mine can never know the love
That draws me to them or the care
That follows them—yes everywhere;
Until to theirs they do transmit,
Their love, can they ere know of it.
So great Mother Nature folds
Us in Her love, the care she holds,
Around our life's primeval hours;
The same to all life trees and flowers,
She holds them in the tiny seed,
Or germ life 'till they can succeed;
And then she holds her loving care,
To still supply them with the air,
That everywhere the world through space,
In orbit goes the air replace,
She holds invariable to fill
The atmosphere with forces still;
That will our life and health supply,
If we with reason will comply;
She makes us feel what is our need
Of elements to best succeed;
That more each individualize,
The more they gain to make them wise
These are the lessons Nature teaches,
What's best for us within our reach,
If we would soon and better grow;
The mind must gather in and know;

Learn all that mind can best express,
And give like freedom to the rest.

IS NATURE CRUEL? NO.

IF no atom ever was void,
  No life can ever be destroyed.
Nature is not expressed in all,
Her united beauty, in this small
Domain of ours, where we may live,
It may be parts where Nature give
To us the thought of selfish power,
Where life some other life devour.
But taken with the whole might be
As some parts of our mind you see,
Might just for illustration say,
Destructiveness might work this way.
Taken as one part, motive power
And this part only see devour;
But if united with the whole,
This part be One—of purest Soul
Combined with others, Nature be,
The kindest mind electrically.
Suppose you lived in Nature where,
Benevolence was only there
To say how kind is Nature seen!
This is kind Nature! true I ween!
You see to know of Nature's Soul
We must combine as One the Whole;

Then we might change our mind and say,
That Nature held not cruel sway.
But we would deem—'twas all life's power,
Of undevelopment the present hour;
That all were on the selfish plane,
Because survival life—would gain.
Life is growing evermore,—
Higher elements explore;
What was once a mystery
Knowledge finds, the causes see;
So the mind in higher states
Of wisdom, learns what life creates,
And in its progress upward climbs,—
Finds out the future home of mind,
And its relationship that draws
Us with connected bonds and laws;
The mind power reaches out in space
Invisibly,—its upward place
Reaches us here, and thought is flown
From minds invisible, are known
The worlds beyond and homes of light—
Their records—have moved hands to write,
In inspiration long ago
And do to-day as all must know.

THE HOLY SPIRIT.

THE Holy Spirit came to man
In all the distant time before;

And now He comes the same to you
As He has come in days of yore.

But 'tis in voices of the ones
We love and they have gone away,
To dwell in heaven's glory where,
There never comes a parting day.

They come to tell you that we live
In all the time that's yet to be;
They come to teach to all mankind,
The truths of immortality.

That's sure to welcome all that live
In fairer worlds of life and light;
And lift the mind to new desires
Out of its own primeval night.—

Darkness in which all growth begins
To upward leap, for air and sun;
So they have come to bring the light
Of purer worlds to every one.

They come when scientific thought
Unfolds the mysteries that were;
And reason dares to search the cause
Of everything that does occur.

And from the lessons of the past
We find life's problem they've begun,
For us to solve and learning more
Of truth for eighteen ninety-one.